Long Shadows

Jan McDonald

Raven Crest Books

ISBN-13: 978-0-9929387-7-2
ISBN-10: 0-99-293877-5

For Bill and My Boys

'OLD SINS CAST LONG SHADOWS.'

Proverb

FOREWORD

Old sins cast long shadows, it is said. But how many centuries can they lay dormant, festering, and polluting, before they are awakened and laid to rest?

In the borderland between Wales and England, where the veil between the worlds is thin and intrusion from the otherworld is commonplace, time has no meaning and the boundaries between past and present are blurred into insignificance.

Restless spirits abound where one country fades into another, feeding the region's folklore with tales of despair and revenge, love and loss, grief and tragedy. Seldom is there found such a tale that ends happily ever after, born in times past when skirmishes and pitched battles for freedom were a part of daily life and border people were never quite sure where their allegiances should lie; their survival often dependant on the whim of the victor.

* * *

CHAPTER ONE: OLD BONES

Geraint Meredith was sweating like a whore in chapel. He wanted to put it down to the exertion of swinging his pick at the cellar floor and being fat, over fifty and well past his sell by date. But this wasn't the warm honest sweat of hard labour; this was the cold, clammy, creeping, crawling sweat of unfathomable dread.

He was used to hacking away at rock, having been a miner man and boy until successive governments had choked the life out of Wales by shutting its pits. It was then he had left the desperation of the Rhondda Valley to become mine host at The Black Mountain Inn, in more affluent Monmouthshire. Megan's old man had conveniently gasped his last and left them 'comfortable see'.

Between the old Hereford road from Monmouth and the Abergavenny to Hereford road, The Black Mountain Inn had stood since the end of the eleventh century. Originally it had stood on a carriage road now long since eaten up by Brookstone Woods. Now it was off the beaten track, with no passing trade but supported by locals and those souls that knew of its location, just a quarter of a mile down a lane from the tiny hamlet of Brookstone.

It had been good at the start, Megan seemed finally happy after God knew how many years. Then she wasn't happy in the bar, she wasn't happy in the kitchen, and eventually she wasn't happy in his bed. Finally she wasn't happy with the poor sod she'd skipped off to Spain with, leaving him with the pub and its debts. And now the pub was dying too.

The fat cat bastards that ran the country talked endlessly of fiscal challenges, credit crunch and double dip recessions, but he knew what they really meant: the country was buggered and he was already seeing how that translated to his takings over the bar.

His plan was to extend the cellar and bring in some of those expensive real ales that might attract the Incomers with their BMWs and posh totty. But Dai Morgan, Dai Bricks to the locals because of his small building business, had quoted him a stupid price therefore making it a DIY job. The truth was that Dai had less desire to be down in that part of his cellar than he did. Mental note to Dai — Fuck you!

The sweating increased and his sparse greying hair was slicked to his head, his shirt was sticking to his back where the cold rivulets of fear were running down his spine and his round framed spectacles were slipping down his nose.

As his pick connected with the floor one more time, the tip disappeared into a void below and a rush of foul air knocked him back.

Bloody marvellous, he'd hit on an old stagnant well or something. As icy fingers closed around his heart and his bowels turned liquid, he knew it was the 'something'. There was bile in his throat and his brain was telling him to leg it back up the stairs into the bar and forget the whole thing, but there was a compulsion that he couldn't comprehend that made him continue to shovel the covering soil and rotten shoring timbers until the entire 'something' was exposed.

He was staring down at a grinning skull, peppered with grizzled white hairs as the scream started somewhere low in his twisting gut, but it lodged in his chest unable to find release as understanding of the black object placed above the skull filtered through the terror.

It was the black cap that had pronounced the death sentence to many in the upper room of the inn. He was looking into the face of Sir Thomas Llewellyn otherwise known as Black Llewellyn, or the Black Judge. In the sixteen hundreds, towards the end of the civil war, The

Black Mountain Inn had been used as a court room and place of execution by hanging. The notch in the old beam at the top of the stairwell still bore witness to its dark past.

The old tales were right, then. Black Llewellyn had been renowned as a lecher and a sadist, pronouncing the death sentence on pitiful folk whose crime had been nothing more than trying to keep their family alive through a hard winter. Those accused of being rebels against the King were summarily hanged without trial, and he was especially fond of hanging the innocent accused of witchcraft. A capital offence, death was mandatory for those found guilty.

Geraint couldn't remember dropping the shovel, or the scream that finally found its way out of his chest, or taking the stairs three at a time, or losing control of his bladder; just his hand shaking uncontrollably as he poured brandy down his throat. He'd slammed the trap door to the cellar shut and bolted it, then stood a heavy chair on top of it.

The third brandy did little to settle him and he thought a fourth would fare no better. What the hell was he going to do? Pull himself together for a start. Maybe that fourth brandy? He realised he was constantly looking over his shoulder.

I mean, they're just old bones. Very old bones. But the eye sockets. Oh God those eye sockets that seemed to be staring back, like black holes filled with something dark and viscous. Like black treacle. Can't leave it like that. Can't call the cops, they'll be all over the place like flies on dog shit. And what about the stuff in the cellar that had avoided Her Majesty's customs and excise? Then there would be the forensics and then maybe archaeologists. Oh God. Gotta fill it back in. Pretend it isn't there.

But it *is* there. Down in my fucking cellar, staring up at me. Mother of God, I'll never sleep again. Christ, I thought it was bad when I had rats down there, but this … This is just old bones. Very old bones. How can they possibly hurt anyone? Because they're *his* bones. Lying there, staring. Can't just leave it, the draymen will be here tomorrow. Gotta cover it up. Can't go back down there. Can't tell anyone. Oh God.

He took a deep shuddering breath that seemed to go on forever, and then poured the fourth brandy. Dutch courage.

He stood looking down at the trap door for several minutes before he could galvanise his body into action. A quick look at his watch told him he had two hours before opening time. Plenty long enough. IT was in a wooden crate, he couldn't even think the word coffin, and his pick had gone through the rotting lid. The soil over the top of the whole thing was less than an inch deep.

A low creak at the foot of the stairs made him cry out involuntarily. *What the fuck …? Get a grip. Old pub, old timbers, old bones, they creak.*

He took away the chair as if it were Dresden china and realised he was trying desperately not to make any noise. He shook his head. There was no-one to hear. Or was there? Maybe …

Geraint Meredith, pull your pathetic self together. Go down there and shovel earth back over the old bones, the very old bones, and forget it. But what if he won't let me forget it? Christ, I'm losing it. He's been dead nearly four hundred years, and been lying down there ever since, he's not going to sit up now and … He felt sick.

His hands were trembling so badly he could only just open the bolt. The trap door seemed heavier than usual as it came up almost in slow motion and he lost his footing on the top step, just catching himself before he plummeted down to the bottom.

Don't think about it. Think about something happy, something clean, untainted by …. STOP IT! Don't look at the eye sockets, keep your eyes on the wall and just keep shovelling. Once those old bones are covered it will be all right. The rest will be easy.

The powers of suggestion are immense and despite all his good intentions he found himself at the edge of the foul grave staring at those deep black eye sockets. And they seemed to be home to something deeply unpleasant, unnatural. He picked up the shovel and slid it through the soil. *Don't look, just shovel!*

The loose dry earth made a clattering sound as it bounced off the old bones, the very old bones, making him stop in his tracks. *I'm sorry. So sorry.*

He leaned forwards over the edge of the rectangular hole and his glasses slid down his sweat slicked nose and before he could grab them, into the gaping hole in front of him.

Ah shit! That's my only pair. Should've listened to the adverts and gone to you know where! The thought made him giggle and he felt better. *Blind as a bat without them, have to get them back. Only one way to do that. Hole's not deep but I just can't reach them. Gotta do it. Don't think about it. Only old bones, very old bones. Christ Almighty!*

He sat on the edge of the hole. Take a deep breath and …

There was a hollow sound as his feet hit bottom, echoing around the cellar. Where were his specs? Bloody dark down there, except for the light from the bar above through the trap door. Daft bugger had left the torch at the top. *Never mind, used to dark holes in the ground.* He tried to visualise where they had fallen. Oh God, up near the head. That gaping, grinning skull. With those eye sockets.

He noticed that he'd stopped shaking. *Good. Got a grip.* It was unexpectedly warm down there, warm for a cellar anyway. And those brandies were beginning to have an effect. He was tired. Warm and tired and strangely sleepy. He felt as if he was nestled in a cosy welsh blanket; the sort his Mam always had over the back of the chair by the fire. Cosy and warm. And tired. Maybe he'd lie down for a minute or two.

There was something not right. He opened his eyes to darkness, he wasn't lying wrapped in Welsh blanket warmth, he was shivering and he was lying on something hard. Something bony. Recollection hit hard. He thought they'd hear his screams all the way back in the Rhondda.

CHAPTER TWO: OLD BOOK

As he grabbed the offending specs he touched something else. What the hell was that? It felt like a book. He shoved his specs back onto his nose hard and squinted through the gloom. It was a book. An old book. An old book with the old bones, the very old bones. Old book might be worth a bob or two. He grabbed it and scrabbled up the side of the pit, coughing bile and recently swallowed brandy.

The thin soil that had lain on top of the … IT … was never going to fill the hole. So he began digging like a demented mole. Digging and shovelling until pain in his chest made him lurch forwards. *Please God, no. Don't let me die down here. Not with THAT!*

He was sweating again but the pain in his chest had subsided so he gingerly tried to stand. He knew he couldn't dig anymore, so he searched around for something, anything, with which to cover the hole. Now he was shaking again. There was nothing. His eyes fell on the old door hanging loose on its hinges, where it had once separated the cellar into two. He lunged at it and heaved. It came away surprisingly easy and with grateful thanks to every God in the known Universe he covered IT. He'd come back later, mix a bit of concrete and seal it back up for good. Plan.

He was up the stairs like a rat up a drainpipe and slammed the trap door shut so hard it bounced back open. He slammed it again and rammed the bolt home like the devil himself was about to come through it. Well, maybe that wasn't so far-fetched.

In the light of the bar he examined the old book. It was thick and heavy about twelve inches square, hand bound in old black leather and tooled with inscriptions he had never seen the like of. The pages were dry and brittle and the writing was a rusty brown and faded. There were diagrams on most pages that made him think of medieval science.

There was an insistent pounding on the front door which made him fall backwards, his mind transferring the banging from the door to the trap door, until he heard Dai Bricks cussing on the other side. "Damn it Geraint, boy, I'm losing good drinking time, isn't it?"

He shoved the book unceremoniously under the bar and looked at his watch; half an hour late! How could that be? It had only taken a few minutes to grab the door and cover those old bones, those very old bones, and even less time to get back in the bar. What …?

More pounding on the door broke his chain of thought, perhaps just as well, it was heading in an unhealthy direction. Geraint stumbled to the door and unlocked it in time to hear Dai questioning his parentage. He shook his head, couldn't afford to lose the few regulars he did have.

"What the hell you been doing boy? Looks like you've been back down the pit!"

Dai's look of surprise and the fact he wasn't already leaning on the bar with his cap pushed back on his head, made Geraint look down at the dirt stained shirt and trousers and his hands.

"Sorry, Dai, been seeing to something in the cellar. Pull your own pint and I'll be back in a minute."

Dai wasn't going to let him go that easily. "Looks like you pissed yourself as well," he said, nodding wisely.

Geraint checked in horror and abruptly turned and left the bar.

"Aye well, if he will go messing in the cellar, specially that cellar. Boy's going to get a bloody fright," he muttered as he pulled slowly down on the pump.

He was seated at the bar in his usual place, cap pushed back on his head, contemplating pulling another when

Geraint returned, looking decidedly cleaner and a little less flustered. He put his empty glass on the bar.

"Better have one with me, boy."

Geraint thought briefly about the four brandies then nodded at Dai. "That's kind of you, Dai. Cheers."

They sipped in silence until the grandfather clock in the corner chimed the hour and Geraint threw his pint everywhere in abject alarm.

Dai sipped on, not commenting or even looking at the landlord, then quietly said, "Been digging in the wrong place, is it?"

He took a step back, cast a nervous glance at the book and felt behind him for the bar stool and pulled himself onto it, shaking again like someone in the grip of fever.

"What do you mean by that? I can't help it if the local builder tries to scam me for thousands. Do it my bloody self."

Dai nodded into his beer. "Well maybe the local builder wouldn't go digging in that cellar for a whole lot more than that. Was doing you a favour, doing it cheap. But maybe now I'm glad you said no."

"Don't know what you mean. Drink it up, next one's on the house for keeping you waiting."

"Aye aye, sounds fair to me. So? Did you?"

Geraint was irritated that his ploy of free beer hadn't distracted Dai. "Did I what?" he snapped. Then held his breath.

"Piss yourself."

The question he'd expected hadn't come and he was so grateful it was a relief to confess to temporary incontinence.

"Yes," he said.

Dai nodded thoughtfully, "Thought so."

And then the lights went out.

Geraint grabbed the bar, frozen rigid. He could hear Dai still sipping his beer. The torch was still at the end of the bar, so he reached out and grabbed it. Flicking it into life and light he edged his way towards the fuse box. The front opened easily and in the torch beam he could see that none of the switches had been tripped. Had to be a power cut, then. They were frequent in the pub.

Except, he could see the lights on across the road in the two farm workers' cottages.

"Damn! Old wiring," he said. *Old bones. Very old bones.*

Dai made no comment, finding the bottom of his glass to be of huge interest.

"Better phone … " Geraint began, but was cut off by a loud fizzing sound followed by a sulphurous yellow glow from the lights, lingering, the colour of putrid fat before they came on at full brightness.

Dai stopped sipping his beer. "Want to talk about it?"

Geraint feigned ignorance, "Talk about what? Drink your beer, man."

Dai shrugged but still didn't return to his beer, piercing the landlord with eyes that drilled for the truth. Geraint's eyes strayed to the old book.

"About what you found when you were digging down below."

"Fucking rats again. That's what I found. Now drink your beer and we'll have no more talk of the cellar. You going to watch the match tomorrow? Gethin Davis looks set for a hat trick, what do you think?"

Dai shook his head, "No, getting past it. Ran like a girl last week."

Relieved that at last Dai was off the subject of the cellar he relaxed and continued to talk endlessly about what the Welsh proudly call 'The Game'.

Then out of the blue Dai said, "How many ghosts do you think there are in this place?"

"Well, let's see, there's the woman that's said to stand over by the fireplace, thought I'd seen her once. Then there's the poor thing that's supposed to kneel at the bottom of the stairs wringing her hands and crying. Never seen her. Why do you ask?" He was on his guard again.

"Just that I heard this TV bloke, parawhatsit, does a programme about haunted places and whether they're for real or not. Just moved in over to Brookstone, I heard. Might be an idea to get him to come have a look."

"No!" The shout was out before he could stop it. "No, not a good idea, Dai. We'll have every nutcase from miles around."

"Be good publicity."

"The kind I can do without, thanks. I think it was done years ago, some medium or other. Came to nothing, and we still have the 'girls' for company occasionally. They don't bother us and we don't bother them. Imprints or something, I think that's what they're called. Recordings like, insubstantial and harmless. Once you get used to them."

"Energy here is funny, it attracts them."

"What do you mean?"

"Dead on the border isn't it? One foot in Wales, the other in England. Weird things happen."

Geraint sighed, "You seem to know a lot about that sort of stuff all of a sudden."

"TV. I heard that bloke say so."

Their conversation was ended by the front door opening to allow two of his other regulars entry. Two lads from the Forestry, both of them from over the border. Delighted at being able to get away from Dai, he was over solicitous to their needs and stayed further up the bar.

At first he wasn't sure if he'd heard anything really, just an impression so to speak. But there it was again. A slow, rhythmic creaking sound, like … like rope creaking against wood.

He glanced nervously at his customers but they all looked oblivious to the creeeeak, creeeeak, creeeeak, that was coming from the stairwell. From the hanging beam.

The door opened again and a tall good looking man came in, ducking under the beam over the door. His hair was prematurely silver and he walked with a pronounced limp. Dressed in jeans and black leather jacket he was , in Geraint's opinion, a handsome bastard with 'incomer' written all over him.

Dai looked up from his beer and raised an eyebrow. "Told you weird things happen."

CHAPTER THREE: INCOMER

Incomer limped to the bar; he had a long scar running the length of his cheekbone which just seemed to enhance his good looks and there was a twinkle in his eye that came from a heady cocktail of general amusement and extreme pain. Mike Travis' Air Force career had ended abruptly when his helicopter was shot down in Afghanistan, resulting in his medical discharge and a leg full of titanium. There had been a short period when he was technically 'dead' and during that time his experiences had led him to his fascination with the paranormal. Looking for answers and explanations had evolved into a passion and a second career that was governed by an open mind and healthy scepticism. It was the latter that had seen him become known as a debunker.

But that was far from the truth as Mike was always delighted to be able to confirm paranormal activity but he left no stone unturned if he suspected a hoax or less charitably, fraud.

It was the twinkle of amusement that connected with a small muscle at the side of his mouth, making it twitch as his entrance into the pub had made him think of the Wild West saloon falling silent when the stranger came through the swinging doors. The silence and interest was palpable even though there was but a handful of people in the bar.

Geraint felt unreasonably irritable but knowing that every customer on the other side of the bar was vital he painted on his mine host face.

"Nice to see you, Sir. What can I get for you?"

Dai had put down his pint and was studying Mike closely. Geraint frowned at him.

Mike grinned at the irritation behind the mask. "Hi. I'll

have a pint of bitter, please."

"Pint of piss more like," Dai muttered.

"That'll do, Dai. Gentleman will think you're serious."

"Aye, aye."

Geraint turned away from Dai, concentrating hard on pouring the pint of beer, unable to prevent his hand from shaking.

Mike perched on a bar stool, "Nice place. I'm looking for a local."

The prospect of regular cash coming over his bar made Geraint more amenable. "Glad you like it. It's quiet though, especially in the week. But you'll be very welcome."

Dai was casting meaningful glances at Geraint and when they were ignored he pitched into the conversation.

"Just moved in over to Brookstone, is it?"

"That's right, Mill Brook Cottage. Word travels fast," said Mike amiably.

Geraint's demeanour changed perceptibly as the penny dropped, but Dai was warming to the situation. "What brings you here then?"

"The wife and I wanted some peace and quiet and I've work in the area."

Geraint bristled. "Work? Not much of that round these parts. You'd be better off up Hereford way."

Mike gave him a quizzical look.

Geraint flustered, "Not that it isn't good to see new faces, course not."

Dai hadn't finished yet. "Seen you on the TV, you're the ghost feller, isn't it?"

Mike nodded and sipped his beer.

"You want to talk to Geraint here, there's plenty of spirits in this pub, and not the ones in the optics, they're on the watery side, if you get my meaning. Isn't that right, Geraint?"

Geraint made it plain that he wasn't amused.

Dai was nothing if not tenacious. "What's the matter

with you, boy? Feller here could make the place famous. Isn't that right, Mr Davis?"

"Travis. Mike." He turned to Geraint who was pretending to be busy at the other end of the bar. Interest from the boys from over the border was growing. TV? The feller must be loaded, maybe stand them a pint or two.

"So, you have resident ghosts, I take it?"

Geraint threw Dai a look that said, *You bastard!* "It's an old pub, bound to be something hanging around, nothing to write home about. Nothing to interest you, I'm sure." He glanced at the old book under the bar, and then out into the hallway where from the stairwell, he could hear the steady slow rhythm of rope on wood. Nobody else appeared to have heard it. *Must be going crackers, because there it is again, creeeeak, creeeeak, creeeeak.* His hands started to shake again. It didn't go unnoticed.

"Not everyone sees 'em, but they're here all right," Dai persisted.

"That's enough, Dai. The gentleman's come for a quiet pint, not to listen to fairy stories."

"Mike," he said. "Call me Mike. And on the contrary, I'm very interested. I'm writing a book about the haunted places on the Welsh English border, maybe I could include the pub?" The twinkle was unmistakeable now.

Geraint had gone pale and the sweat was noticeable on his brow, he was certain he could hear movement in the cellar. A sort of clattering noise, like dry earth on … *old bones, very old bones. Oh Jesus.* He was sweating profusely now. He wasn't religious but he mentally crossed himself.

Mike finished his pint and fished about in his pocket then pushed a small card across the bar, "If you change your mind, give me a call. The address is wrong now, but my cell number's the same. Any time."

Geraint looked at it as if it was radioactive. He forced a small laugh, "Go on with you. The only spirit in this place worth talking about is the twenty year old malt. Maybe you'll come and try it one day."

"Maybe I will," Mike replied affably.

Conversation was commonplace for a while as Mike finished his pint, which despite Dai's remark to the contrary was extremely good.

"You keep a good cellar," he said to Geraint.

"*What?*"

Mike studied the landlord for a second or two. "You keep a good cellar." He nodded at his empty glass. "The beer is good."

Comprehension and relief flooded Geraint's face. "Oh, right. Thanks."

Mike stood up and nodded. "Well, better get going, or the wife will be messing about moving heavy boxes and the like."

Dai's interest piqued again, "Wife? Didn't know you was married." Then as he pondered Mike's remark the proverbial light bulb came on in his head. "Expecting is she?"

Mike beamed with pride as if he were the only male to ever have achieved such a feat. "Yep. Eight months. We'll just have to time to settle in."

Dai was muttering something into his beer about *that* cottage.

Geraint was relieved to see that Mike was heading for the door. "Nice to see you, Sir," he said again. "Welcome to you and your good lady."

Mike raised a hand in farewell, "Thanks. Oh and by the way, the old lady over there by the fire is a might agitated. She's pacing up and down and looking very worried."

Geraint dropped Mike's empty glass and it shattered around his feet. All eyes were on the fireplace but could see nothing.

All except Geraint whose eyes were fixed firmly on the trap door; he could see. He could see old bones, very old bones, and two filthy black holes that were staring up at him.

CHAPTER FOUR: NEW LIFE

In the middle of the chaos that was 'moving home', Beth stood between boxes in front of the old mirror she'd found in a Monmouth junk shop. Her hand strayed to her swollen belly and she gently stroked the sheltering infant. The mirror reflected a golden flash from her wedding ring, bringing a broad grin to her elfin features.

Beth Travis, she thought, *Mrs Mike Travis. I wonder how long it will take to get used to being called that?*

A sudden pain at her temple made her start. The memory of the events in Crowsmoor was never far away, and a simple thought would always send her spiralling back there. She shuddered and shook her head as if to dislodge the images. She believed now that Crowsmoor had truly been cursed, and it had cursed her. No matter how many miles she put between them, those memories would always haunt her.

Leaving Crowsmoor without a backward glance had been impossible for Beth as she had paid a last visit to the burned out remains of St Michael's. The churchyard was empty but far from quiet. She had heard the ghostly tolling of the six o'clock bell wafting on the ether as if Charlie Paynter himself was bidding her farewell, telling her not to worry, it was still his watch. But a new life waited for her, a new life with Mike and their child, a return to an old life, as she had found peace and solace in a meaningful blend of her old beliefs and Christianity without the Church.

Having been brought up by pagan foster parents for a considerable time, she had grown to love the Goddess and the Horned God of the forests. That is, until those loving foster parents had been killed and she had bounced back into the system, ending up eventually with a couple who had balked at her pagan ways and beaten them out of her, sending her reeling into the church where she had drifted into becoming one of the first politically correct female vicars. That life was now firmly buried with a padlock and chain attached.

Neither she nor Mike had enjoyed living in the city and they soon began searching for the peaceful cottage that they both yearned for. It had taken six months to find it, but now they had, it felt as if they had lived there forever.

A Tudor black and white, extended over the years, Brookstone Cottage nestled in the narrow valley along the Mill Brook in the picturesque hamlet of Brookstone. Placed between Monmouth and Hereford it was an ideal location for Mike's work, now centred in the borders between Wales and England. From the moment she had seen it with its For Sale sign she had felt at home. It was the first time she had felt this, ever, and when Mike agreed, it was a done deal.

Mike's first offer had been accepted without negotiation and they couldn't believe their luck. Now just ten months after leaving Crowsmoor she was home.

A cup of chamomile tea was in order before tackling more of Mike's boxes. There would be time later to sort out junk from treasure but unpacking was a priority having almost fallen over two boxes already. She was eternally grateful that he would now have a study where all his books, notes, and equipment would at last find a home.

Brookstone Cottage was long and narrow, hugging the bank as it fell away from the old Hereford road, and all of the leaded windows faced south so that the whole cottage was filled with spring sunshine by day and now, at night, the ethereal light of the moon as it hung low over Brookstone Woods. She stopped as she passed the bedroom window looking out over the garden to the brook, when a sudden pain in her temple made her gasp. She rubbed it hard and squeezed her eyes tight shut in an effort to banish it.

As she opened them a movement in the garden caught her eye. A young woman stood near the brook, her mahogany hair long and sleek, framing wide dark eyes and a sad expression. And then she was gone.

"You up there, Wife?" Mike's voice from the bottom of the stairs brought reassuring warmth, making her forget both the pain and the woman. It seemed an eternity ago that he'd limped irritatingly into her life, constantly amused by her, seemingly mocking her and then it had all changed.

She heard his footsteps on the landing and frowned momentarily, still worried about the narrow period staircase in the cottage causing him pain. But he'd been stubborn. They had both fallen in love with the place instantly and he'd insisted it wasn't a problem, saying his titanium knee and ankle could climb Everest, but still she worried. She forced it away and turned to face him with her usual smile.

"I like this mirror here, what do you think?"

He laughed at her as he stood behind her and hugged her to him, "I think you're getting fat."

"Seriously? I thought it was just the mirror needed cleaning. Are you sure?" She peered comically into the dusty glass.

Her laugh always sounded like it came from some other place, some other world and would eternally entrance him. Together with her otherworldly features, dark hair and eyes, it was her laugh that always got to him.

"Did you find the place?" she asked him.

"I did. And I was right, it's well worth including in the book, but I'm going to have to win round the landlord first. He's one edgy character. There's more going on there than I could see. Although I did see an old lady very briefly. She was looking more than upset and quite a lot peed off."

"So it was worth it then. What's the pub like?"

"Full of character and history. *That* I can get from the locals and the internet, but I want his co-operation. I can't publish without his consent, well technically I can, but I won't. Come downstairs and I'll make coffee and tell you all about it."

She wrinkled her elfin nose, "How about some tea? I've had too much caffeine today already." She rubbed her belly, "She'll be awake all night as it is."

"You're really sure she's a she?" he teased as he took the stairs in front of her in case she fell.

"I am. Now, tell me about the pub."

"Patience wife, I'm trying to tell you. It's one of the oldest pubs in Wales with loads of history to the place and according to my preliminary research, endless reports of ghosts, ghoulies and long leggedy beasties going back years. Though he denies it. Probably bad plumbing or loose floorboards for the most part."

"But?"

"But there was something, I don't know, something 'off'. If you know what I mean."

Unfortunately she did. She sighed but it had an affectionate smile behind it. "Let's have that tea and then you can help me finish the unpacking."

He guided her backwards until she plonked down onto the sofa. "Sit!" he said with a grin as he made for the kitchen.

She settled back against the soft cushions and closed her eyes. She felt like a contented cat as the moonlight fell onto her face.

A sudden shadow crossed before her closed eyelids and she blinked them open abruptly, expecting to see Mike in front of her with a steaming cup, but then she heard him whistling in the kitchen. Without knowing why, she crossed to the window and there it was again, that sudden and persistent pain in her temple. And there *she* was again. The beautiful young woman standing by the brook and looking directly at her. Beth raised her hand in greeting, a neighbour perhaps, used to walking freely along the side of the brook? But at this time of night? The woman made no movement in response, just continued to stare at her.

She called out, "Mike!"

He was there in seconds, arriving at the same moment that the woman was gone. "Beth? What is it?" the panic in his voice obvious.

"I'm sorry, love, I didn't mean to scare you. It's just … it's nothing; I thought I saw someone in the garden that's all. She's gone now."

He sat her back against the cushions again and crossed to the window, peering out across the overgrowth of grass and weeds, *Got to get to grips with that fairly soon,* scanning the garden and seeing no-one.

"Must have been a trick of the moonlight, honey. There's no-one there."

The whistling of the kettle interrupted further conversation but he could see she was unsettled, *overdone it probably,* he thought. He brought the steaming cup of her favourite chamomile tea and kissed her on the forehead. "I'll go and have a proper look, it may be a neighbour come to say hello."

She smiled, of course he was right, her nerves were frayed from the move and the excitement of their new home. That thought settled her and filled her with welcome warmth. Their home.

She saw him pass the window and disappear out of sight as he pushed through the tall grass down towards the brook where she knew he would find no-one.

He returned minutes later with concern creasing his brow. "No-one there. Put your feet up and stay there. Maybe have a cat nap? I'll go finish unpacking. I don't want you throwing out my old junk when you think I'm not looking," he teased.

She snapped back at him," I don't need a 'cat nap' as you put it! I'm pregnant Mike, not ill!"

He inclined his head slightly and the tell-tale twitch at the corner of his mouth connected with the twinkle in his eye. The same twinkle that had originally irritated the hell out of her, that now just brought an answering smile.

"I'm sorry, love. And don't *dare* say a word about hormones or you will be in real trouble," she laughed.

He shook his head in mock horror, "Wouldn't even dare to think it!"

Still, he had a point. She was tired and hadn't been sleeping well and for every box they unpacked there seemed to be five more to deal with. And with the shimmering silver rays of the moon over the garden and the backdrop of Brookstone Woods seemingly alive with the gentle late night breeze, it had probably just been a shadow or as he said, a trick of the light.

But why didn't she believe that?

CHAPTER FIVE: TWO BLACK HOLES

It was closing time and for the first time that he could recall, he was reluctant to see Dai Bricks get up from his place at the bar, pull his cap down onto the front of his head and say his usual, "Right then, best be away isn't it? Nos Da, Goodnight."

"Fancy a lock in?" Geraint asked him tentatively.

Dai narrowed his eyes. "Not like you, boy. Something bothering you, is it? Maybe something in that cellar of yours?"

It was enough for Geraint, "Suit yourself, Dai, I was just offering, that's all. Get yourself home then."

Dai nodded at him, hesitated for one hopeful minute, and then apparently made up his mind to leave. Geraint's hopes fell flat.

The door closed behind Dai, last to leave as always, and now he was on his own again.

Except it didn't feel like it.

His heart was pounding as he locked the door and cast a wary glance towards the fireplace. *No old girl there, maybe that Travis guy was full of shit; maybe he'd heard some of the old tales about the place, fishing for more information. Yes, that was it. Well, he'll get nothing from me. There's nothing amiss with the pub. Nothing for him to write about anyway.*

He went to turn off the lights and found that he couldn't bring himself to do it.

Crossing the room he picked up a heavy oak bar table and struggled with it behind the bar, thumping it down onto the trap door with its bolt firmly in place. *Must get a padlock for that tomorrow.*

At the foot of the stairwell he turned to look behind him, then made a sudden dash across to the bar and grabbed the old book, the old book that he'd found with old bones, very old bones.

He was at the top of the stairs before he could breathe and in his bedroom slamming the door and leaning against it, his heart threatening to break through his rib cage.

He looked around the room and everywhere that his eyes settled had Megan written all over it. Bitch. Leaving him after all those years for a younger bloke with a tight bum and a beard. Poor sod. Well, he'd go into Monmouth in the morning and buy some paint and maybe even a new bed. He didn't know why he hadn't done it ages ago when the divorce had been final. The thought calmed him down, his bitterness and anger at his ex-wife was a good purgative for the cold fear that had settled somewhere deep in his gut. He breathed out again. And while he was in town he'd call in and see Bill Jenkins in the antique bookshop on the High Street. The old book might bring him enough to pay for his bedroom makeover.

Comforted by the possibility, he undressed for bed then frowned. It was a lonely place these days. He hadn't noticed it at first, relieved to be rid of the constant whining and nagging, but for all that she'd been a comforting warmth beside him on cold nights. Now there was just a cold space next to him. Bitch.

He started for the bathroom, but the prospect of leaving his bedroom and crossing the landing, walking past the beam, the beam that had the notch in it from the constant pressure of the hangman's rope, made him change his mind.

He got into bed and opened the old book. It had been written in Old English with the odd page or two in another language that he thought was Latin. The pages were thicker than he'd noticed at first, brittle with age but they weren't made of paper. *Parchment. That was it, parchment. By God Geraint boy, maybe you'll get enough to take a break somewhere. Just a weekend, like.*

He turned the pages slowly, studying each one as if he

understood the strange symbols and diagrams. The musty smell that had pervaded the old book seemed to have lifted. *Good, don't want anything to detract from its possible value.*

He yawned, more tired than he'd thought. But he was relaxed now, warm under the feather quilt and warm inside at the prospect of …

Creeeeak.

He sat bolt upright.

Daft sod. All that talk about stuff that really shouldn't be talked about and the shock of finding … Get a grip boy, only old bones, very old bones.

Creeeeak.

He was out of bed and pressed against the wall.

What the hell was that sound. Almost like … like someone breathing heavily outside the door. Outside my door, for fuck's sake!

He stared at the door, not breathing but desperately wishing he'd visited the bathroom before climbing into bed. He stared hard at the door handle, willing it to remain still. *Don't turn. Don't turn. Oh God.*

The sound of the night breeze was in the room with him then, as it blew the net curtain billowing into the room. He allowed air to enter his lungs. *Christ I need to stop watching bad late night movies. Get a grip; it's just a night breeze.*

Even so, he'd leave the light on.

He tried to turn his thoughts to his prospective windfall. There was no question of ownership. He owned the pub; therefore he owned what was *in* the pub. *Including the old bones. No, don't think about that. Concrete over it tomorrow and forget it.*

Sleep came eventually through sheer exhaustion, although it was the kind of sleep that broke easily. The slightest sound would wake him.

And it did.

He'd been dreaming about two black holes. Two black holes that were staring up at him from a skull that wore a black cap. His pillow was damp with sweat as he strained to listen.

There it was again. The sound that had woken him from the clammy grip of his nightmare. A scraping sound. *What the hell was it?* His mind struggled to make sense of it. It sounded like something heavy being dragged across wood.

Old wood that covered old bones.

He was wide awake then, alert in all his senses. The familiar silence of the pub draped itself around him. Too sensitive by half, he was. Megan used to say that. Well, he'd prove her wrong.

He got out of bed and went to the door, listening.

Nothing.

He put a hand out to the handle, noticing that it was trembling. *For God's sake!* He stared at the handle as if it would suddenly come to life and snatch at his hand. Then in a sudden movement he grabbed it and yanked the door open.

The landing sprawled before him in its familiar black emptiness. Nothing there. He moved to the top of the stairwell. Nothing.

Two steps down, then another two, and another two. The hallway below sheltered nothing spectral, just the old hall table with the Aspidistra, Megan's Aspidistra. Mental note – Get rid of that tomorrow as well.

In the corner of the bar, the grandfather clock told him it was almost two o'clock. He was going to be knackered in the morning.

The bar was still lit up like a Christmas tree so he walked boldly through the doorway. A brandy would settle his shattered nerves and help him get some sleep. Now he thought about it, there were still some of Megan's sleeping tablets in the bathroom. Brandy and a pill should sort him out, lull him into dreamless sleep.

He moved behind the bar and took a glass from the shelf. Reaching out to the optic he stopped dead in his tracks, his flesh crawling away from his bones, blood draining from his face and fear removing all thought except the one that was screaming at him.

The table that he'd shoved on top of the trap door was now several feet from the offending aperture and the bolt was drawn back.

CHAPTER SIX: OLD FRIENDS

Beth had hardly slept, unable to get comfortable, she had tossed and turned all night and the baby had kicked her constantly over her bladder which had resulted in several visits to the bathroom.

Mike on the other hand had slept soundly, muttering reassuring words to her occasionally and at other times snoring softly like a contented kitten.

The spring sunshine was pouring through the old leaded window panes filling the cottage with the promise of bright things to come as she padded into the kitchen to make tea. There was a prettily wrapped package on the worktop with a small card and a huge kiss drawn on it.

The contents tinkled as she unwrapped it carefully, finding inside a beautiful set of wind chimes with a pewter medallion of Mother Mary hanging central to the tuneful tubes. Delighted, she immediately went to the kitchen door and stepped out onto the crazy paved terrace. The cherry blossom was in full bloom, clustered pink along its branches as she hung the chimes onto a low bough and they immediately began to sway and chime.

"Housewarming present." Mike stood watching her from the doorway, a broad grin on his face. "Pretty, aren't they?"

She threw her arms around him and planted a massive kiss smack on his lips.

"Mm, let's see? What else can I bring you?" He hugged her tightly, and nuzzled her neck. "Now, wench, breakfast. A man has to eat before facing the day."

She frowned momentarily, "And the night," she said softly. "Promise you'll be careful."

"It's what I do, honey. And the advance on the book

paid the deposit on the cottage. Besides, it's an old abbey, some trust or other now. What harm can I possibly come to?"

"Don't say things like that!" she chided him. "You should know better by now, not to put that kind of thought and energy out there. I love the wind chimes, Mike, thank you." She treated him to another hug and big kiss on the cheek.

Before she could ask him what he wanted for breakfast his phone was ringing and he had disappeared into the heart of the cottage.

"Mike Travis."

"Hi, Spooky. Croeso Y Cymru. Welcome to Wales. Settled in yet?"

The voice of his friend Jack Carter made him smile as his friend addressed him by the nickname he'd endowed him with.

"Hi, Jack. Finished the unpacking late last night, bloody garden's full of cardboard boxes. Don't think Beth's noticed them yet."

"How *is* that beautiful wife of yours? Blossoming, I gather. You don't deserve her. Life is so unfair."

Mike laughed. "Yeah, right, in case you hadn't noticed, she's got the wrong chromosomes to interest you."

An answering chuckle came from his phone. "I thought I'd drive over one evening, bring a bottle or three. When was the last time we got together?"

"When I was single."

"Well, there you are then, you denied me the honour of being best man, buggering off to Gretna to get married over the bloody anvil."

Mike was delighted to hear from his friend. He and Jack had trained together in the RAF as helicopter pilots and had served together in the same squadron in Iraq and Afghanistan. Jack had come out unscathed but Mike had been unlucky and copped for a massive crash when a spray of bullets had brought his chopper down at the perimeter of the camp and he'd hit the deck hard while thankfully having just taken off. He'd *'Gone for Six'* in RAF slang, *Brown Bread*, *A Gonner*, but the highly skilled medics immediately on the scene had worked on him and eventually resuscitated him, the result being a year of surgery and rehabilitation with his left leg full of titanium before medical discharge and a pension. What he thought of as his 'other problem' was the thing that drove him in his new career. He had been technically and physically dead for twenty minutes after the crash but instant medical attention ensured that when they eventually got his heart started again there was no brain damage. Just an acquired knack of being able to see 'ghosts' from time to time.

Jack had snatched the MOD's hand off when they were flashing great redundancy packages around; enough to persuade the bank to finance the start of his business, running helicopter charter flights out of Cardiff Wales Airport, mostly ferrying businessmen to and from the City. Good on, Jack. Mike had been genuinely pleased for him. It would be good to be able to catch up and maybe see him again from time to time.

"Want to take a bird up sometime?" he asked Mike.

"Love to. You know I only hold the Class 3 licence now? I was lucky to be able to keep that too."

"Sure do, but you've still got to keep your hours logged in, mate or you'll be handing that ticket back too. Any time. You know that. So, what about the weekend, I'll be good and I'll bring flowers."

"Sure, Beth is looking forward to meeting you. Friday?"

"I'll be there. Straight out of Monmouth on the Hereford road, right?"

"That's right. See you then."

"Toodle Pip, old bean," Jack quipped.

Beth was leaning against the open door jamb, watching him. "Jack?"

Mike nodded. "Jack. He promises to be good and bring you flowers."

She smiled, liking his friend already even though she hadn't met him. "I'm really looking forward to meeting him. When?"

"Friday."

"Mike! That's only two days away!"

"Yeah. Problem?" Corner of his mouth twitching.

"Yes, problem. I need to get the spare room ready if he's going to stay and get a nice meal and …"

Mike put his finger over her lips. "And I'll see to the spare room when I get back from the abbey, and I'll sort out dinner. And yes, I know I'm a lousy cook, but there's a brilliant invention called a takeaway. Jack will love it. And he'll love you. So stop fretting, wench. And I think the toast is burning."

Beth turned back hastily to rescue the offending bread as Mike's phone rang again.

It was Gavin St. John Radford, manager of the abbey for some trust or other. He always used his full handle and Mike disliked his pompous attitude but was careful not to show it. He needed the guy's say so on several of the trust's properties that he wanted to investigate for his book but he also knew that Gavin wanted the free publicity from book sales. He'd been waiting for the call for days, for the okay to proceed at the abbey. He hoped the eleventh hour call was the news he wanted to hear.

"Good morning, Mr. Travis. Gavin St. John Radford speaking. I'm calling to advise you that permission is granted for you to investigate the abbey, subject of course to the conditions that we have already outlined with regard to your equipment."

"That's great news, thank you." He pulled a face at Beth, crossing his eyes and nodding into the phone. She laughed aloud.

"I'm sorry?" The Radford voice was decidedly icy.

"Er, sorry, the radio. So, I can make my way over there today as arranged?"

"I just said as much, did I not?"

"Thanks. Just wanted to clarify."

The sniff at the other end indicated that when Gavin St. John Radford made a statement there was no requirement for clarification.

CHAPTER SEVEN: RUBY

Geraint Meredith hadn't slept either, not since he woke at two o'clock anyway. He'd spent the remainder of the night huddled in a corner of the bar, too afraid to return to bed and too afraid to turn his back on the trap door to the cellar, and too afraid to turn his back on those old bones, those very old bones.

He stared relentlessly at the trap door defying it to move, heart stoppingly, breath holdingly afraid that if he took his eyes off it, when he looked back it might be open and he'd see those black, sinful eye sockets staring from underneath the black cap.

The grandfather clock struck the hour, the eighth hour. A bicycle bell sounded outside followed by a rattle of the front door. Ruby! God, he'd forgotten Ruby, his 'lady that did' as they say. She was a cheery forty something, who tried without a whole lot of success to look twenty something, with overflowing cleavage, peroxide hair and skirts that were too short when she *was* twenty something. Many a cold bed had been warmed by Ruby, or so they said. It had never occurred to Geraint. Until now.

She was the daughter of old Maggie 'Mam' Thomas from Old Brookstone Farm over Brookstone way, and Ruby lived in an old farm workers cottage alone, her husband having decamped many years previously with a mousy woman from Hereford. True love, it seemed, had long eluded Ruby.

She came in every morning at eight till nine thirty and saw to the bar and washed the bar towels, tidied his living room up the stairs and made him a cup of coffee. How the hell could he have forgotten Ruby?

He slid up the wall keeping his back pressed firmly

against it and edged his way over to the door, keeping his eyes fixed on the square of timber in the floor behind the bar.

Ruby pushed open the door as he released the lock and bolt.

"Morning G … Bloody Hell! You look God awful; I'll make you a coffee while you get in the shower. You and Dai Bricks have a lock in?" She breezed past him in a haze of cheap perfume.

Geraint stared after her, wondering why he'd never appreciated her voluptuous curves before and then mentally debated how she would … What the hell was wrong with him?

Ruby's presence and the spring morning sunshine made him feel better and then a little foolish. A grown man cowering in the corner all night in case … in case the trap door to the cellar opened.

That was it, enough was enough. First thing after coffee he was going to the out of town retail park and coming back with sand and cement to cover over the old bones and that would be that. Job done.

Ruby surpassed herself with coffee and toast; she obviously felt sorry for him. The dark circles around his eyes, gaunt face and general twitchy behaviour must have sparked a crumb of pity somewhere.

He wasn't in the mood for her usual constant chatter about nothing in particular lightly peppered with local gossip, and tried to tune her out. Her conversations were usually one way affairs anyway.

He sat in the bar near the fireplace, as far away from the bar as he could manage, concentrating on his toast.

"… Mam said. And she's pregnant, not long to go, either."

"Hm?"

"She's pregnant, about eight months Mam said."

"Who? Who's pregnant?"

Ruby sighed. "Sometimes I think I'm talking to myself,

Geraint Meredith. His wife, of course!"

Geraint frowned, "Whose wife?"

"You haven't heard a word I was saying, have you?"

No. I was more interested in the top of your thigh
when you just bent over the vacuum cleaner.

"I'm sorry, Ruby. I'm a bit distracted this morning."

Distracted by your very ample thighs.

"What was it you were saying?"

Then you can bend over that vacuum cleaner again.

Ruby obliged, turning it off so that Geraint could focus
on what she was saying, consciously shaking his mind to
be rid of the uncharacteristic thoughts.

"That Paranormal feller from the telly. Handsome he
is, shame about his limp. Moved into Brookstone Cottage
he has, him and his wife. She's pregnant poor lamb. Bet
she doesn't know what she's in for. And he doesn't look
like he's up to middle of the night feeds and all that with
that limp. Not that men are any bloody use like that
anyway. Have their use of us and let us get on with it. I
wouldn't want to be that close to someone that messes
about with that sort of thing anyway, stirring up trouble,
Mam says. What do *you* think, Ger?"

I think you'd warm up that cold patch in my bed.

He said, "He was in here last night. One pint wonder.
Didn't stay long, I think Dai put him off. I think he came
to nose about, looking for a story that isn't here."

Ruby put a hand on her ample hip, "What are you
talking about, Ger? There's plenty to interest him here.
Mam says there's an old lady always stands over by the
fireplace *and* there's a weeper, bottom of the stairs. Mam
says …"

"Yes, well, I've got to get to town. You can let yourself
out the back door, Ruby. I'll leave your wages under the
bar."

Under the bar … there was something else under the
bar. Something that might be valuable. Something that had
been with the old bones.

Ruby sensed his lack of interest in her daily news and bent to flick the vacuum cleaner into life.

Then stood up with shriek.

"Geraint Meredith! What the bloody hell do you think you're playing at you old bugger?"

Geraint was perplexed.

Until he realised that he was holding more than a handful of Ruby's generous backside.

He pulled his hand away as if it had been in dipped in acid, his eyes were wide and he was sweating again. *Jesus, what was happening to him? Must be going senile, turning into a dirty old man. But I'm not old, I'm not. I'm not like that, ask anyone. Ask Megan. No, don't ask Megan.*

"God, Ruby, I'm so sorry. I ... I don't know what came over me, I ..."

Ruby's demeanour changed suddenly and her eyes were alight as she sidled towards him, "Getting lonely of a night here, is it? Fancy a bit of company now and again? You should have said."

Geraint was terrified. Not terrified like last night, but terrified of Ruby and the way she was looking at him. He made for the door, hearing Ruby's throaty laugh following him from the bar.

CHAPTER EIGHT: THE WELSH WAY

The day ahead stretched lazily in front of Beth. Mike was off doing an investigation into the paranormal activity, or lack of it, at the old abbey and wouldn't be back until the following morning. When he'd either return bleary eyed and tired or wide eyed and animated, depending on the paranormal activity, or lack thereof.

Half way across the living room, she stopped suddenly, her hand flying to her temple. The pain was there and gone again before she could register it. Instinctively she went to the window.

She was there. The woman with the long mahogany hair. And there was a feeling, like things being out of kilter. Just like the first time she'd seen Fenn Dawson in the graveyard in Crowsmoor. But Mike hadn't seen her. And it was Mike who had the faculty of seeing through the veil, not her. She shook her head to clear it and opened the French doors and stepped out onto the crazy paving.

She raised her hand to the woman. She could see her more clearly in the morning sunshine, dressed in a long dark red skirt over a white linen shift, and a tightly laced black bodice. Beth was hesitant to make further moves in case she vanished as she had the night before, leaving her no room for debate about the nature of the woman.

At which point she did exactly that.

Beth stood quietly assessing her emotions. There had been no feeling of malice from the woman and there had been no interaction between them, but she had definitely been staring at Beth. Time to discuss it with Mike, now she was sure. Sure she'd *actually* seen what she'd *thought* she'd seen.

She sighed and smiled simultaneously. She knew what

it would mean. Tape recordings, thermal imagers, magnetic field monitors or whatever they were called. He'd be like a terrier with a rabbit until he either saw it for himself or could prove activity scientifically. You'd think after Crowsmoor …

She shook the memory away; today wasn't the day to dwell on that place. Today was the day for connecting with their new home, maybe do a little blessing, relax and let the cottage speak to her. Get to know each other.

Maybe take a little walk, not too far, or wander through the high grass to the brook, connect with the water energy and any water spirits there.

Her comforting thoughts were brought to an abrupt end as the doorbell rang.

Padding softy to answer it she was puzzled as to who it might be at such an early hour. They knew no-one in the area and there were no immediate neighbours, the nearest being in Brookstone itself, in the huddle of cottages that straddled the Mill Brook.

But these were country folk and country folk as she had soon learned had their own way of doing things, be it in Cornwall or the Welsh border. She didn't doubt that their arrival, accompanied by the removal van with 'City2City Removals, London' emblazoned on it, had caused comment at a few dinner tables along with derogatory remarks about 'Incomers'. They were prepared for it, and prepared to prove themselves 'worthy'.

On the doorstep stood a tall, spare woman, with iron grey hair pulled tightly into a knot at the nape of her neck; the sort of woman that defied any guess at her age. She wore a long skirt and old fashioned blouse, both covered with a floral apron with straps that crossed over at the back. She had a weathered face with pinched, stern features, a sharp hooked nose and eyes that you just knew missed absolutely nothing. It was those hawk-like eyes that fixed on Beth.

"Good morning," she said in a voice devoid of

expression other than the soft welsh lilt that was somehow mellowed with Herefordshire.

"Good morning." Beth scanned the woman, looking for a basket with clothes pegs or bunches of heather.

The woman shook her head. "No, they're up to Hereford way at the moment. Won't bother you none, anyway. They don't stay around here much with better pickings to be had the other side of Monmouth."

Beth was flustered, she hadn't meant offence but the woman had apparently read her thoughts. And even more flustered when she realised that she did indeed have a basket which was on the flagstone beside her.

"Mam Thomas," she said as she held out her hand. "From Old Brookstone Farm. Just come to say welcome, that's all."

Beth took her hand; it was warm and felt like old soft leather. She stood aside, "That's so kind of you, please, come in. I'm Beth Travis."

"Aye, I know. Well, I haven't come to stay, just to bring you a few eggs from the hens this morning, and some milk from Agnes. Tide you over, isn't it. 'Till you can get sorted."

"Er, thank you, that's very neighbourly of you." Beth thought of her well organised and extremely well stocked kitchen.

Mam Thomas raised an eyebrow. "It's the Welsh way."

"I was just about to make some tea, please come in and have a cup with me. I'd like that," she said impulsively. "I must say we'd heard that incomers into Wales were often not welcome."

"No, that's *North* Wales. Well, just a cup then, I've chores to be doing on the farm." She stepped inside the cottage and fixed her beady eyes on Beth's necklace.

"No need of necklaces and folldirolls in my day, you just got on with it and used what was around you. Pretty though, I'll give you that."

Beth put a hand to her silver pendant of the Goddess

holding a moonstone; a wedding gift from Mike. "Got on with what?"

"The Craft. Got it in you, I can see. Can't hide it if it's in you. I said so to Ruby last night. Got it in her I said, sure as eggs are eggs. It's not in our Ruby, though. You can't put it there if it's not there to start with, see."

Beth felt as though she was expected to know who Ruby was, so didn't comment. Mam Thomas had followed her into the kitchen, taking in every minute detail. An inspection; the welcome was the excuse.

"Eight months, is it?"

Beth nodded and unconsciously put her hand on her belly.

"You're carrying low. I brought you something." She fished into her basket and brought out a jar of dried herbs.

Beth's heart sank. Memories of Nan Bottrell in her madness made her feel unsteady. She could do without that, but she had to be polite to her new neighbour.

"Raspberry leaves?" she queried.

"That's right. See, I knew you had it in you. I said so last night."

"To Ruby."

Mam Thomas ignored the unspoken invitation to explain who Ruby was, so Beth took a wild guess. "Ruby's your daughter, right?"

"That's right. Only one."

"How long have you lived at the farm?" Beth had no idea even where the farm was, but it perpetuated polite conversation.

"All my life. I was born there and I'll pass there. Four generations of Thomas's have lived there, see. Though it's not as big as it was; my grandfather sold a parcel of it off, just left with the meadow and the barns now, the hens and Agnes. But it's enough for an old body like me to deal with."

Beth had the distinct impression that even when life was extinct, Mam Thomas would still be at Old

Brookstone Farm.

"Well, now, I'll be going. If you need anything, I'm always round the farm."

"Thank you for the eggs, and for coming round," said Beth, genuinely pleased to having apparently passed inspection by the old woman, for some illogical reason it seemed important.

On the threshold, Beth blurted out, without prior thought, "I suppose you know quite a bit of the history of this cottage."

Mam Thomas spun around, hawk eyes glinting, piercing. "Why?"

"Oh, I just thought it would be nice to know about who had lived here previously. It's Tudor, well the original cottage is Tudor, and so it must have plenty of stories to tell."

The hawk eyes didn't give an inch. "Oh yes, plenty of those," then after a moment or so, "You've seen her haven't you?"

CHAPTER NINE: SHADOWS OF THE PAST

BROOKSTONE 1645

Owain forked the last of the turf over the smouldering wood pile which was the size of a small room. He dare not take his attention away from the charcoal burning as flames might rise in the heart of the pile and all the charcoal would be ruined. Despite it being a late winter day he was hot and dry from his labours. He dipped a cup into the pot of water and drank it down in thirsty gulps.

His was a solitary life, living and working in the woods, tending the charcoal night and day and a time of great uncertainty amidst political and religious turmoil. With Charles I set to lose the war against the parliamentarians, once again Wales would be thrown into upheaval. The question of loyalty to Anglican or Catholic meant little to most of the rural Welsh, who discretely remained true to their pagan heritage, attending church only because failure to do so could mean their necks or a hefty fine, but most remained loyal to the King.

Owain was able to be absent from church because of his work making him unable to leave the fires unattended, and the fact that Monmouth Castle demanded most of what he produced. The witch frenzy that was raging in England had little effect so far in Wales but word of Matthew Hopkins, the Witchfinder and his abominations had filtered across the border and folk were forced to conceal their religion and their practices for fear of swinging at the Assizes.

Sir Thomas Llewellyn, Black Llewellyn as he was known, had become renowned for his zealous pursuit of witches, as he labelled the local pagans, midwives and herbalists, along with rebels against the King. All who usually ended up in the court room on the first floor of the Black Mountain Inn where the local Assizes were held. Those accused and found guilty of either crime, often without trial, ended up swinging by the neck from the hanging beam at the inn.

Most of those accused of witchcraft were simple folk who were close to the earth and her ways, understanding the potency and power of herbs as healing agents and living in harmony with the ebb and flow of seasonal tides and the life cycles of their deities. Many were accused simply because they were involved in personal feuds with neighbours who knew that to accuse the other of witchcraft was a sure way to be rid of them.

With Charles on the brink of defeat, the Royalists were scouring the countryside recruiting as many men as they could commandeer into the King's army. Owain had so far avoided such a fate as his camp in the woods was practically impossible to find. Even the rising smoke from the smouldering wood was difficult to follow through the dense forestation.

He had first met Adain when she had wandered into the clearing on the festival of Imbolc, February 1st, when she honoured the Goddesses Brigid and Cailleach. On this day she collected wood for her hearth fire from the deepest part of the wood, symbolising the warmth and light that would come from the darkness of winter and welcome in the spring. It was a lean time for gathering herbs but wood sorrel could always be found. She practiced her pagan religion alone and the woods provided perfect concealment for her as she honoured her Goddess and God away from the eyes of Black Llewellyn's men whilst gathering herbs for her potions that would damn her as a witch if discovered.

The weak winter sun was fingering its way through the bare trees into the clearing when she had wandered into his camp. Her mahogany hair was crowned with a garland of snowdrops and she was humming softly to herself.

He was suddenly conscious of his soot and smoke smeared face and his grubby hands.

"Oh," she said. "Good day. I'm sorry if I disturb thee."

He was flushed with work and heat from the fire but he felt himself flush a deeper red.

"Good day, Mistress" he replied awkwardly. "Art thou lost? The paths through the woods are hard to find."

Her laugh sounded like the Mill Brook bubbling over the granite rocks. "No, I am not lost. I know the woods well enough, though I rarely venture this far. She held up a basket half full with leaves. "I was looking for some wood sorrel which grows sweeter in the deeper parts of the forest."

"Aye, I know of it and I know where there's a goodly crop growing. I can take thee there." He cast a glance at the smouldering woodpile, calculating how long he would be away. "Thou art versed in the healing arts?"

"Be thou a King's man?" she asked anxiously.

He laughed as he spread his hands and looked down at his rough tunic. "I am Owain ap Rhys and I am a charcoal burner."

Adain smiled at him and he felt as though the Midsummer sun had suddenly illuminated the clearing. She smiled demurely at him, "Well, Owain ap Rhys, my name is Adain Powell and you may show me the goodly crop of wood sorrel if it pleases you."

It pleased him immensely.

She came daily after that meeting, sometimes bringing him soup or stew in her basket, and he in turn would provide cider traded in Hereford for sacks of his charcoal, or they would cook a rabbit over the fire.

They had grown together in easy friendship until Beltane on the first of May when they became lovers under the canopy of the trees in the flickering light from the Beltane fire.

Beltane was the time to call in summer and acknowledge the union of the Goddess and God. It was a time of great feasting and frolicking for larger gatherings and young couples intent on mimicking the lusty activities of the Goddess and the Lord of the Forest.

Adain scraped a living from spinning and dying wool that she gathered from hedgerows and gorse bushes or traded from sheep farmers at Monmouth market, exchanging her herbal remedies discreetly for a fleece or two. Her cottage had been gifted to her mother who had been nurse to the children of Monmouth Castle, until it changed hands three times during the civil war that raged throughout the country. Then her mother had lost her life to the deadly fever despite all her ministrations and Adain had settled into the cottage alongside the Mill Brook where she practiced her healing arts learned from an old man at the castle when she was young.

Owain could not leave the woods and Adain could not leave her cottage, but they were married at Midsummer in the heart of the forest in the joyous pagan ritual of Handfasting. Owain would come to the cottage and stay for a few days after each burning and trading in Monmouth. Then they would part for him to return to the wood and begin burning the next load of charcoal.

News came to him only when he loaded his cart with the charcoal and took it into Monmouth to the castle and the market at the end of each month, or on occasion when he journeyed to Hereford to trade his charcoal for cider. On his last trip the news was of Cromwell's army, led by Thomas Fairfax, being victorious in the Battle of Naseby, effectively ending all hope for the King.

Cromwell, they said, was marching towards Wales.

CHAPTER TEN: THE ABBEY

St Winifred's Abbey was an hour's drive away, squatting at the foot of the Black Mountains, small as Abbeys go, but Mike's first glimpse sent a frisson of anticipation down his spine which he immediately strove to dispel. It was no way to begin an investigation. Above all else he had to be objective, clear headed and free of any preconceptions.

Despite his own previous experiences.

Research into the history of the place was standard along with records of eye witness accounts, but above all he had to be open minded halting just on the edge of the precipice of scepticism. It was a fine balance which he had mastered early on, thanks in the most part to his past military discipline. He would conduct the investigation from the beginning, talking to the eye witnesses, walking around the abbey just taking it all in before setting up his equipment.

As he stepped out of his Volvo automatic his leg was stiff and the pain shot right up into his lower back. He hadn't driven far but unpacking their boxes late into the night had taken its toll. He frowned, the last thing he needed at the start of the investigation was pain that would distract him from the smallest event or detail.

He threw a Tramadol down his throat and swallowed hard, smiling at the thought of Beth who cringed when she saw him do that with no water to swallow the tablet. It sometimes still seemed surreal, him and Beth. He had gone to Crowsmoor in Cornwall in answer to a request for help from an old man and soon found himself in a web of deceit, murder and paranormal activity. And Beth.

Thinking of Beth and the image of her, as close as if she had been right there with him, made him smile. Jack

51

had been right. *Mike Travis, you are one lucky bastard.*

She had been the vicar of Crowsmoor and a fish out of water. He'd been attracted to her from their first meeting and the terrors that had followed had only served to convince him that he wanted to spend every day and night with her.

She had an ethereal quality, slim, dark hair, dark eyes and elfin features. And now she was having his baby. A girl she said, with clear conviction, refusing the midwife's offer of confirmation when she had her scan.

The thought of his child brought a fleeting pang of regret. She, if Beth was right, would grow up knowing no grandparents. Beth had never known her real parents and after the death of her beloved foster mother and father, had essentially grown up alone. His mother had died from a particularly aggressive cancer that had started in her bowel and rapidly eaten up the rest of her in a matter of months. His father, well, best leave that stone unturned. They hadn't spoken for over ten years.

Further thoughts on the subject were halted as a tall figure emerged from the abbey. The man was well built and athletic, all suit and latest iPhone. His walk was more an overconfident swagger and he had a knack of looking down his aquiline nose as if someone had placed something unpleasant underneath it.

It could only be Gavin St. John Radford.

Mike was aware of the appraisal as the man approached.

There was no 'Hi, I'm Gavin,' or even 'Good morning', it was the barest nod accompanied by "St. John Radford, please come this way, Mr Travis. I have made the necessary arrangements and you will be able to speak to those who claim to have seen the … manifestations, I believe that is the best description." He cast a glance at Mike's leg as he limped forwards, hand outstretched. Ignoring the proffered hand he asked coldly, "Do you require any assistance with your equipment?"

"No, thanks, I'm fine. It's good of you to meet me here. Thank you for your time. I'm sure you have better things to do."

It was plain that the St. John Radford agreed wholeheartedly. It was a more than generous gesture on his part. Mike smiled and his eyes twinkled as he delved through the cool exterior, the guy wanted the free publicity, otherwise there would be no investigation at the abbey and despite the look of indifference bordering on total disinterest, he felt there was a hint of curiosity buried deep and safely under control.

Mike slung one of his bags over his shoulder and followed him into the abbey.

Caught up in Henry VIII's dissolution, the abbey had been empty for several decades afterwards, but unlike the more remarkable ones such as Glastonbury, it had survived and had been restored back in the seventeen hundreds. Its life cycle had been abbey, empty, restored private dwelling, school, convalescent home, and now it was in the hands of a trust. Enter Gavin St. John Radford, the manager of said trust.

The interior of the abbey was surprisingly light and airy with beams of morning sunshine streaming through a dome of glass at the top of the stairs which Mike suspected was a late addition during the eighteenth century. He followed Radford into the library, a pleasant oak panelled room, typical of its nature.

"So, Mr Travis, we understand each other with regards to the conditions of access to this property."

Mike nodded. "Sure. Anything that I write regarding the abbey you have first sight of and right of approval. My equipment must not be obtrusive or damaging to the fabric of the building in any way. That goes without saying. I have twenty four hours to conduct my preliminary investigation with the option to return the following day, should my findings require it. I think that was about it?"

Radford drew himself up to his full height, all six foot

three of it, appearing to try and inflate himself like one of those puffer fishes.

"Please don't forget that the upper east wing is the victim of eighteenth century dry rot and the timbers and floors are unsafe. Insurance and Health and Safety require us to keep it locked off. Other than that you are free to investigate wherever you wish. I expect you to respect the property in every way, and also the housekeeping staff who you wish to interview. I think that is all. I'll leave you to it then, the key to the main door is in the lock. Should you need to leave the abbey before morning, please lock the door behind you and put the key back through the letter box."

He handed a brown envelope to Mike. "This is the scaled map of the building that you asked for. It's a copy, obviously, so you may use it however you wish." From inside his briefcase his produced a worn leather volume of obvious age and placed it carefully on the desk. "You may find this useful. Now, depending on the outcome of this preliminary investigation the other members of the trust will be guided by me with regard to further investigations of other trust properties."

"Thank you. I'm particularly keen to look into reported events at Marston Manor. Erm, can I ask you a question? Why now, when permission has consistently been denied and I wondered if you personally have seen or heard anything here."

Radford raised an eyebrow as if to say that if he had by chance seen anything of a paranormal nature, there was no way that he was going to discuss it.

"That's two questions. I shall look forward to reading your report, Mr Travis. Good day."

He was out of the door and into his brand new BMW in short order. Mike smiled at the image of the St. John Radford coming face to face with Eleanor, the Blue Lady, reported as having been seen on the main staircase. Probably ask her not to wear out the carpet.

Most of his equipment was packed into two custom made cases, sitting inside snug fitting foam rubber for protection. He hauled the cases from the back of his car and placed them carefully onto the ground while he pulled out several collapsed tripods to hold his various camera and devices. With these under his arm and a case in each hand he trundled them into the library having decided to use that room as a base for his investigation.

The return trip saw him return with a laptop and a box filled with spare batteries; these places had a habit of sucking the life out of them. In much the same way as they sucked the life out of their residents.

In the library, Mike unlocked his main equipment case and began putting the pieces on the desk that sat centrally in the room, dominating it with its size and heavily ornate carving.

The Electro-Magnetic Field meter had been his first purchase along with his digital camera for capturing still images. The EMF meter would indicate any changes in magnetic fields which are believed to indicate a possible spirit presence. This would be his first piece of equipment used as he walked through the abbey obtaining baseline readings in every room especially around electrical appliances such as televisions, radios, computers, microwave ovens and refrigerators.

He would repeat the operation with the digital infra-red thermometer. Cold spots were also a good indication of spectral appearances.

His latest treasure was a thermal imaging camera that had cost the best part of six grand and had been a gift after the last TV programme, compliments of the Producers, part of his salary deal. He patted it, almost gloating over it, he would not have been able to afford such an investigative luxury but it was definitely a wow piece of kit.

He slipped a small digital voice recorder into his pocket to record the readings as he did his preliminary walk through.

A nervous cough outside the library door announced the arrival of Mary, the youngest of the staff at nineteen, a part time cleaner.

Mary was short and decidedly obese which probably accounted for her breathless demeanour. She wore a shapeless T-shirt over an equally shapeless long skirt. Mike smiled at her warmly.

"Hi, come on in. You must be Mary," he said, mentally referring to the names provided by the St. John Radford.

She nodded and entered the room apprehensively.

Mike nodded towards the old brown Chesterfield. "Take a seat Mary, get comfy, I won't bite."

He had won the girl over with his second relaxed smile. She was about to hang on his every word, even though it was she that was supposed to be doing most of the talking. She plumped down heavily onto the cracked leather.

"I'm Mike," he said quietly, "And I think you know why I'm here and why I need your help?"

Again with the nod. Mary was obviously going to be economical with her words. Time for a different tactic.

"The thing is Mary; I really need your help. I've never been here before, in fact I'm new to the area, and I need all the help I can get with this investigation. So anything you can tell me would help me enormously."

Mary's adenoidal breathing increased and she looked up into Mike's eyes. He smiled encouragement at her. "How long have you worked here?" he asked.

Mary seemed to be trying to work something out but was obviously struggling. Then she brightened.

"Since I left school. Been here since then," she said.

"It's very big responsibility, keeping a beautiful place like this clean and tidy. You do an excellent job."

Mary flushed. Mike felt like a heel, flattery was not in his nature but he felt Mary had something to say and wanted to say it and that would need all methods of persuasion.

"Do you work here every day?"

She shook her head. "No. I gets a day off every Friday. Sometimes on Sunday. I goes to Church on Sunday. I'm a good girl." She frowned.

Mike smiled with genuine warmth. "I can tell that. It's why I want to talk to you first. Because I know that you won't be telling me any fairy stories. You'll tell me the truth. About anything spooky you've seen around here."

Mary laughed. "Mrs Evans said you were on the telly. I've never seen anyone that's been on the telly before."

"Well there's absolutely nothing special about anyone that has been on the telly. Especially me. I've given that up now anyway, I'm writing a book instead. And I want to write about the abbey. So, have you seen anything or heard any noises you can't explain?"

"What like her they calls the Blue Lady? I've seen her a coupla times, only on the stairs though. She don't say nothing, just walks down the big stairs and then goes into the drawin' room. She's never in there though if I goes to look. But I'm not scared of her. She's kinda pretty. She won't hurt me. I'm a good girl, I am."

Mike made a mental note of her concern that he should think she was 'a good girl'. He put the thought into a box file in his head and carried on chatting to Mary about the Blue lady, who he supposed was possibly a residual image, an imprint in time and place recorded in the ether and replayed at intervals, regular or otherwise.

"Has the Blue lady ever spoken to you?" he asked.

This idea caused Mary to laugh loudly, her mirth taking over, making her snort. Eventually she said, "Oh no, she don't never speak, she's a ghost. They can't speak."

Mike wasn't about to disabuse her of the comfort in that belief.

"Course, there's the woman in the crypt that screams, so they say. I ain't never heard her. And I won't go down there. I got a bad row about that first off, cause it's supposed to be me that cleans down there."

Mike was horrified at the idea of innocent Mary being

57

exposed to such an environment, but maintained his warm expression.

"Who cleans down there now?"

"Mrs Evans." Mary sniffed, "She don't like me, says I'm stupid and too slow, but I told her, I might be a bit dull but I'm not so dull as to go down there and she could sack me if she wanted."

"Good for you, Mary. Was it Mrs Evans that you had the big row with?"

"No, it was him that's in charge here. Him that comes in a suit and posh car."

Gavin St. John Radford.

"But you didn't get the sack. You stood up for yourself and I think that's great. You should be proud of yourself for standing up to him." Mike grinned, genuinely proud of this young girl, socially challenged and none too bright, who hadn't bowed before the throne of Radford.

Mary flushed. "I knows my place, and I should've done as I'm told, cause I'm a good girl. But I was scared, see."

She bowed her head in case Mike agreed with her that she should have done as her superiors had bid her.

Mike leaned forward in a conspiratorial fashion, "Tell you the truth, Mary, I'm a bit scared too."

"What? You?"

"Yep, me. I sometimes get scared in dark creepy places. It's nothing to be ashamed of."

"I ain't done nothing to be ashamed of," she said abruptly.

No, Mary, I don't believe you have, because you are a good girl.

"Of course not. I just meant that lots of people get scared from time to time."

Mary took on the look of an overweight frightened rabbit. She jumped to her feet. "I gotta go, see. Mrs Evans said I wasn't to be long. She said I got jobs to do and not to waste your time."

He smiled and stood up, putting out his hand to her.

"Well, thank you Mary, you've been a great help. If you want to talk to me again, I'll be here until tomorrow lunch time and then I'll leave my phone number in the book in the hallway."

"I was really a help? I ain't never been a help before." She seemed pleased and nervously taking Mike's hand for a brief moment she hurried breathlessly out of the door.

Her hand had been slick with sweat; Mary was clearly very anxious about something and had obviously been glad to leave. He wondered what she hadn't told him.

A sharp clack clack from the flagstoned hallway prevented further thought. The estimable Mrs Evans. And she was not what he was expecting.

Mid thirties, model slim in an expensive dark grey suit that probably cost the best part of his annual pension, immaculately made up in stuff that hadn't come off the shelf in Boots and even his naïve eyes could see the shoes were hand made, Italian leather probably. She clacked into the library on a heady waft of Coco Channel. She was in fact every inch, **not** his idea of a housekeeper. He did a quick reassess.

She bore down on him in a business-like way, more suited to the boardroom that the housekeepers parlour. He frowned as he tried to picture her with a feather duster and vacuum cleaner down in the crypt. It wouldn't gel.

"Mr Travis, I'm Mrs. Evans, Housekeeping Manager. I understand I am to give you every co-operation in your … investigation."

She looked at Mike in a way that would have curdled the proverbial milk. Mike smiled, invoking the twitch at the corner of his mouth that betrayed his amusement.

"Hi, yes please that would be very much appreciated. I won't keep you long; you're obviously a very busy lady." *Down in the crypt with your feather duster and vacuum cleaner.*

"Before we commence," she said dryly, "I would ask you take anything that Mary may have told you with a pinch of salt. She is, shall we say, intellectually challenged and has been blessed instead with a more than average imagination. She does sometimes get carried away. Now, how may I be of help to you?"

Mike was under no illusion that any help he was going to get from her would be a matter of public knowledge and no more. He kept the questions short and neutral. Had she seen anything that could be described as paranormal? Had she heard any unusual or unexplained noises? Had she ever been there at night? *Had she ever smiled?*

As he had surmised, she was as tight lipped as a criminal waiting for his lawyer. No, no, and no. *And no.*

"I've read reports of an apparition described as The Blue Lady. Is there any fact behind the legend?"

"Eleanor. The wife of Hugo De Montefort who bought the abbey and made it into a family home after the dissolution. She's been seen by several people on the stairs. Though how much of it is coloured by local folklore, I don't know."

"I assume you employ other cleaning staff as well as Mary?"

"Yes, there's Ruby Thomas. She works on a part time basis but she called in sick this morning. It's a shame you won't be able to talk with her. If Ruby has seen anything she would be more than happy telling you about it. Then we have a bank of casuals that come in prior to functions along with regular catering staff most of which double up on the housekeeping bank. Gavin said you would probably get what you need from the regulars so we haven't included them on the list."

He noted the 'Gavin' and the 'we'.

"Never mind, another time perhaps." He watched her carefully; her mask gave no sign of cracking.

"Indeed. Well, if that's all?"

He nodded, almost glad to be out of her company. Something about her made him shiver. But then, she was the kind of woman that made him shiver. "Thanks, you've been a great help."

She had in fact. He was now convinced that there was something going on at the abbey that they didn't want discussed. Even though they had given him permission to investigate the place.

Hang on. Perceptions clouding judgement. Had to clear his head of that notion to be able to do a proper investigation.

He sat for several minutes, clearing his mind, pulling in light, steadying his breathing. A technique he'd developed over months of lying in pain in hospital beds, techniques learned thanks to the formidable character of Dion Fortune, whose book Psychic Self Defence had somehow landed on his bedside locker from the hospital library trolley. He smiled at the thought 'somehow'. In his previous life before the crash, it would have been coincidence, but now he knew that 'coincidences' weren't random. The book had become his touchstone, his Bible, during the long dark months when he was trying to make sense of what had happened to him. In the accident and afterwards. It was this book that had gone some way to his understanding of what may have happened at that time. He thought about it now. And frowned at the questions it didn't answer.

Whilst he knew that objectivity should be his watchword during any investigation, he also knew that so called gut feelings usually emanated from the subconscious mind and generally should be listened to.

As far as the investigation went on the eye-witness front, it was down to Mary, unless he could get more from locals and the 'casuals'. He mentally shook off his line of thought.

Time for his walk around.

CHAPTER ELEVEN: EMPTY HOLE

Geraint was half a mile down the old Hereford road before he realised that he had forgotten the old book. *The old book that had been buried with the old bones, the very old bones.*

He cussed mentally and decided to carry on to the out of town DIY superstore for sand and cement. He didn't want to go back to the pub while Ruby was still there. He shook his head, embarrassed at the memory of what he'd done. He didn't know what had come over him. Best thing was to stay out of Ruby's way and when she arrived in the morning, just carry on as if it hadn't happened.

But it had happened and he couldn't get it out of his head.

He threw the paper sacks into the back of his car and checked his watch, ten o'clock; Ruby would be finished at the pub and gone. It was safe to go back, concrete over …IT, and then get a stiff brandy. Afterwards he would take that old book into Bill Jenkins in the High Street; it was bound to be worth something.

Feeling more relaxed he wound the car window down, it was a warm sunny morning and the earlier stress had given him a headache. Blow the cobwebs away, get ready to do what he had to do. Then he could forget it.

Maybe.

He pulled up in front of the inn, no sign of Ruby's bicycle. He heaved a relieved sigh.

It didn't take long to mix the concrete, enough to cover the old door that he'd put over … IT. He was sweating hard though, as he finished shovelling the grey sloppy mixture into an old wheelbarrow. He planned to lower it into the cellar from the drayman's door on the side wall. He stopped dead; he hadn't put the planks up the stone

63

steps.

Unlocking the padlock that held the chain through the two door handles, the chill of the cellar washed over him. It was probably his imagination, but it seemed darker than usual down there. There were no windows in the cellar, but with the doors open there should have been more light. Instead, the darkness had coalesced into something solid, something tangible, and it seemed to wrap itself around him.

And it made him feel sick.

"Hi, Ger. Lovely day,"

The voice scared him witless and he shot upright, cracking his head on the low beam. "Shit!"

Brian Jervis the drayman took an involuntary step back. "Bloody Hell Ger, you gave me a turn."

"*I* gave *you* a turn! Christ, Brian, you nearly gave me a heart attack! Stupid bugger. Think I've cracked my skull. What the hell're you doing here at this time anyway? Lunch time is the usual delivery time."

"Sorry? Er Ger it twelve o'clock mate. Usual time. You okay?" He looked concerned at Geraint's pale face and the shaking of his hand as he gently rubbed the top of his head. He nodded to the wheelbarrow of cement.

"Need a hand with anything, Ger? Glad to help."

Geraint felt the blood drain even further from his face. No way. No way could he let them down in the cellar, not until …

Geraint's head reeled. Twelve o'clock, that must mean … two and a half hours gone. And he hadn't moved from the spot. He'd been standing there, doing nothing, standing there while the darkness wrapped itself around him. He shook his head to clear it.

"Fancy an early lunch, boys? Free pint, while I just do a little job down there." His voice was unsteady.

Brian looked at his watch and shrugged, they'd have a pint off Geraint anyway, always did, but they were on schedule so a leisurely lunch appealed. He grinned at

Geraint and nodded at his partner. "Looks like I'm blowing the whistle. Come on."

Geraint scuttled ahead of them throwing on the pumps at the main switch and pouring two pints of best. It was the second occasion that he'd apparently lost time, been oblivious to its passing and no recollection of doing anything within that time. It could be serious, maybe he had epilepsy; he'd heard that epileptics sometimes became oblivious to time like that. Or maybe he had a brain tumour.

Maybe he should get on with the grim job in hand and then worry about bloody brain tumours.

The boys were settled next to the fireplace with their pints and complimentary crisps. "I'll be down the cellar, won't be long. If you finish your beer before I'm done, help yourselves to another. Only one, mind!"

The thought of a second free pint in the offing brought a broad grin to Brian's face. "You take your time, Ger. We're fine here." His partner nodded his agreement.

The fleeting thought of how this would make Megan angry gave Geraint some small comfort. She was always going on at him about giving away their profits. Well, sod you, Megan.

He grabbed his torch, made a mental note to get the electrics down there sorted and took a deep breath before opening the trap door behind the bar and letting it slam back against the floor. It was still too dark down there, a dense dark that seemed to be somehow alive.

Don't be daft. Imagining things now. Probably the brain tumour.

He descended the stairs through the thick darkness, unwilling to look over at IT, keeping the torch beam directly ahead of him. Allowing for its erratic movements as his hands shook, that is.

The planks leaned in their usual place against the wall opposite the drayman's steps. He placed the torch on its haunches while he deftly laid the wood against the steps, ready for his wheelbarrow and the new barrels just delivered to roll down into the cellar. He'd have to keep a firm hand on the barrow, the descent from outside was steep.

Geraint clambered up the planks, not wanting to go back into the bar and disturb the boys in case they got nosy. Making it to the top with several splinters he hauled himself into the outside air, half expecting a sucking noise as the darkness tried to cling on.

He lay for a moment at the top of the steps, puffing like a good'un. He really had to get more exercise.

Eventually, he pulled himself upright and got a good grip on the wheelbarrow. The torchlight looked as though it was fading. Or was it just getting darker down there?

Very slowly and deliberately he wheeled the barrow onto the planks and leaned back, trying to counterbalance the momentum of it, straining to keep it slow. Gradually, inch by inch, he brought the barrow to a halt at the foot of the steps. He exhaled loudly.

He picked up the squatting torch and frowned, it was definitely getting dimmer, and he only put new batteries in it the day before. Still, it wouldn't take him long. Straighten up the old door and tip the concrete on top. Level it off with the back of his spade and job done. When it was dry it would take all hell to shift it. He wouldn't even have to look down into the hole.

The torch flickered. He shook it and it got brighter and steady.

The old cellar had originally been divided into two parts and he negotiated the opening in the centre, now minus its door. The wheelbarrow was heavy and he was glad to set it down next to the hole.

The empty hole.

Geraint screamed, and the torch went out.

CHAPTER TWELVE: THE OLD BRIDGE

Beth was staring at the retreating figure of Mam Thomas through the hall window, shaken at her last question and finding herself unable to answer it. She felt safe behind the door and refused to think about the implications of the conversation that had ended so bizarrely. She just wanted the old woman to be gone.

She watched as she stopped at the garden path and fished something out of her pocket, fiddling with whatever it was before carrying on up the path to the gate. Beth frowned as she thought she saw the old woman sprinkling something as she walked. At the gate, her suspicions were confirmed as Mam Thomas bent down and deliberately spread whatever it was back and fore. She stood upright slowly, betraying the arthritis, and looked steadily back at Beth before walking away without a backward glance.

Beth had the door open and was half way up the path in seconds, bent forwards, scanning the path for whatever the old woman had scattered there. A glisten of white made her stop, puzzled. She crouched down with difficulty in the most inelegant of positions as she allowed space for her large belly between her knees.

She picked up some of the white crystalline substance from the top of a stone, squinted at it, and then gingerly lifted it to the tip of her tongue.

Salt.

Mam Thomas had laid down a path of salt and crossed her outer threshold, the gate, with it too. Creating a seal. The old woman was afraid of her and had created a barrier against magic, containing any magical work that may come from her or the cottage.

Beth was annoyed. Whilst she was part pagan in her

beliefs, she didn't hold with any occult work against another. She returned to the house and into the kitchen where her broom stood bristles upwards behind the back door. She took it immediately outside and began to brush away the salt, scattering it, clearing the old woman's spell as she brushed. At the gate she brushed the salt out into the road. The next rain would wash it away completely.

How dare the old woman come and visit her then cast a spell on her as she left?

Her annoyance didn't diminish after she had cleared the salt and she knew that she was about to take it out on the breakfast dishes.

As she walked down the path back towards the cottage a pain in her temple made her gasp and her hand flew to her head. She spun around to look for the woman who would be standing down by the brook.

She wasn't there.

The pain in her temple faded into nothing as she stared at the spot where she had previously seen the woman, who now she knew to be not of this world. A cool breeze wafted across her face, stroking her hair, soothing her ruffled feathers. She smiled as she felt herself calming.

Mike hadn't seen the woman, which meant that either she hadn't been there and Beth was hallucinating or she had been there but had only wanted to be seen by Beth. She didn't know how that would work, and wondered if Mike would know more. She had seen ghosts before and in Crowsmoor had collaborated with them to keep an evil spirit at bay.

She slipped off her shoes and stepped onto the grass in front of the house, treading lightly, enjoying the feel of the warm earth under her feet as she wandered slowly down to the place where she had seen the woman on the previous evening.

The brook was bubbling and dancing over the granite outcrops, creating white froth where the water bounced against the rocks. She mentally greeted the water spirits as the morning sunshine threw rainbows over the dancing water. Of the woman there was no sign. Nor had she expected there to be.

Her annoyance at Mam Thomas had lessened to some degree as she returned to the cottage intent on tea and a favourite chocolate digestive. She wondered how Mike's investigation was going and wished he was there with her.

The kettle was quick to boil and Beth poured the steaming water into her favourite teapot, enjoying the fragrance of the tea and the soft sound of the water as it fell into the pot.

As she replaced the kettle, she became aware of another sound coming from the living room. It was a faint and rhythmic whirring sound interlaced with a repetitive click. The sound grew louder as she entered the room and she stood stock still trying to pin point the source.

It seemed to come from a spot in a large alcove next to the fireplace but as she stood there, it grew fainter until it vanished completely.

It was a very old house and all old houses had their sounds and settlings and she would soon get so used to them she would no longer 'hear' them. She smiled at the thought. After all, it was what she had planned for the day; getting to know the house and allowing the house to get to know her.

The hot tea lifted her spirits as she lay back on the sofa, wriggling her toes and stretching her legs, keeping things moving below her swollen belly. Swollen belly had seemed synonymous with swollen ankles from quite an early stage in her pregnancy and like all mothers to be, she would be glad when the pressure was off them.

As she sipped her tea, taking pleasure in dunking the chocolate biscuit, the whirring, clicking sound came again from the same direction. She frowned, unwilling to get up from the comfort of the sofa to investigate the sound further. A glance at the wall showed no electrical sockets and no obvious heating pipes; although she knew that there could be both wiring and pipes under the floorboards. The sound seemed to be too rhythmic to be of either origin and the central heating pump was off.

The tea and warmth of the sun on the sofa enhanced her natural fatigue and she felt her eyes closing. Unwilling to fight the impulse, Beth allowed herself to drift pleasantly into sleep.

It was a strange sensation, one of looking out of someone else's eyes. At some higher level she knew she was dreaming but the dream had a surreal quality as is she was living it through another. It was hot and sticky but her tread was light and there was pure joy in her heart. She carried a basket over her arm, its contents covered by a white linen cloth and there was a name on her lips. Owain.

She was in her own garden although it looked very different from how she now knew it. Everywhere there was a riot of colour and the air was filled with the heady fragrance of herbs and sweet flowers and the steady drone of bees about their business. Their home was an old fashioned straw skep at the bottom of the garden at the edge of the brook.

As she stepped lightly towards the corner where now grew a huge hydrangea she saw a small wooden bridge spanning the brook and joining with a well trodden footpath into the woods.

There was another feeling too, a familiar sensation, it was how she felt when she had first learned of her pregnancy. Delight, excitement, pride and an overwhelming protectiveness tinged with awe and wonder.

She crossed the bridge lightly and had begun humming a tune she had heard the minstrels play in Monmouth Castle when she had lived there as a child. The name came again. Owain.

The footpath quickly became shaded as it led into the depths of Brookstone woods and she was glad of the cool breeze that ruffled the leaves and played in her hair. The woodland herbs that thrived in shade were abundant but she barely gave them a second glance as she quickened her footsteps, eager to get to her destination to feel his loving arms around her and to see the light in his eyes when she told him her news.

Her basket was heavier than usual as she had made fresh lemonade, unwilling to drink the potent cider that Owain had brought back from Hereford and she had traded a batch of medicines for a pig's carcass. She had roasted half of a leg glazed with honey from her bees and had baked Owain's favourite Bara Brith, the traditional Welsh fruit bread. It was a day for a celebration.

The trees and undergrowth were dense as they drew her towards the heart of the woods, to where she could begin to smell the charcoal wafting on the morning breeze, to Owain.

She made no sound as she approached the clearing where his hut and his stacks of charcoal and the charcoal pit stood, declaring his presence and his trade, but he was aware of her presence before she could speak his name.

He took her tightly in his arms and kissed her deeply before she rested her head on his broad chest, dwarfed by his athletic and muscular frame, savouring the familiar scent of smouldering wood that always clung to him.

"I have tidings, my dear one," she said. "And I have brought a goodly repast by way of celebration."

He looked into her radiant face and she had no need of further explanation. His face wreathed in a smile that was as broad as he was.

"A child? We are to be granted the gift of a child?" His voice was thick with emotion and despite his size he felt the need to sit on the soft bracken, pulling her with him, unwilling to let her go. "When is this to be, my sweet wife?"

She giggled girlishly, "Why, don't you remember the last time that you were home with me? I wouldst hope that you hadn't forgotten that sweet night."

He laughed at her mockery. "Why surely how could I

forget. It is the memory of you that keeps me alive whilst we are apart."

She kissed him gently on his roughened cheek, "Our child will be born at Candlemas. A gift from the Goddess indeed."

He frowned as he looked down at her heavy basket a censure on his lips but before he could speak she placed her finger on his mouth, "I am with child, not sickening of the fever. I shall know when it is too heavy for me to carry to you."

She prevented further argument by laying out the white linen cloth directly onto the bracken and covering it with the roasted pork and Bara Brith along with chutneys and pickles that she had laid down the previous autumn, shaking her head as he gestured towards the stone jar filled with the strong brew of cider.

"I have lemonade," she whispered, "I cannot partake more of the cider until after our child is safely born, perhaps some small beer which I shall brew directly. The first brewing I will bring to you and shall share what remains with others in the hamlet."

He nodded his understanding and replaced the heavy stopper into the top of the jar after taking a hefty swig from it. "A child," he repeated, "A child at Candlemas."

They spent the remainder of their time lying in the bracken, watching a few white tendrils of cloud in the otherwise blue of the summer sky. Midsummer was almost upon them and there would be double the celebration. His face clouded over as he pondered the long periods he would be spending away from her, punctuated only by her daily short visits to him until he was ready to take his charcoal to market again, when he would spend some nights with her before returning to the clearing to repeat the cycle of charcoal burning once again.

She read his thoughts and smiled at him, "We will be well, dear one. We must thank the Goddess that you have labour to sustain us. It is enough."

Beth awoke with a start, the scent of the wood smoke still in her nostrils. The sun had lost its midday heat but she was overly hot and flushed as she struggled to her swollen feet, laughing quietly to herself as she pictured Mike and his mock effort as he pulled her up from the sofa.

Her first instinct was to go into the garden, now overgrown and edged with a tangle of willow herb and brambles. She made her way through the long grass once more, carefully picking her way towards the left hand corner where the hydrangea had asserted itself and gone wild. It was the place where she had seen the girl on the previous two occasions. She half expected to see her standing there but she was alone in the garden.

The hydrangea had grown taller than Beth and was almost as wide as it was high, effectively concealing what lay behind it. Beth pulled at a few branches until she could see through the giant shrub.

It was there!

The small wooden bridge, blackened by centuries of bitumen. It was perfectly preserved, but was it safe?

She pushed her way around the hydrangea and stood looking with a growing excitement. Maybe she should wait for Mike to make sure it was safe. But there could be no harm in having a closer look.

She put one foot tentatively onto the platform of the bridge, accompanied by a loud creak as the bridge showed its surprise of a human foot after so many years, but didn't move or show signs of imminent collapse. Maybe just a step or two? How many feet had crossed the bridge in the past? Where were they going?

"Hello!"

Beth jumped in alarm at the voice that had brought her back to reality.

Spinning around so quickly she almost lost her footing, she found herself looking at a very pretty woman, possibly in her late thirties. She was wearing a navy blue nurse's uniform and carrying a small leather bag.

"Oh, God! I'm so sorry. I didn't mean to startle you. Are you okay? You shouldn't be putting yourself in danger of falling, you know," she added, nodding towards the old wooden structure. "I'm Kath. Kath Dickinson, the district midwife. I was just having a coffee with your neighbour. She told me you'd just moved in and were heavily pregnant. Thought I'd call in and say Hi."

Beth's confusion lifted and she beamed at the woman. "Hi. I'm Beth Travis. I haven't had chance to register with the local GP as yet, planned on doing that tomorrow. It's good of you to call. It looks as though the jungle drums have been beating, then?"

Kath laughed, "Sure. This is the country, Beth. Get used to it. Its harmless enough, people just taking care of their own neighbours."

Beth stepped carefully off the bridge and held her hand out to the midwife who took it enthusiastically.

"Come inside, and let's have some tea," Beth said with a smile.

CHAPTER THIRTEEN:
DISAPPOINTMENT

There was still a chill in the air, despite it being late May but Geraint was sweating. Not the cold, twisted sweat of fear like before, this was different. He was nervous.

He glanced down at the book in his hand; this thing could be the turning point for him. Maybe at last, he could spend some cash on doing up the pub. Maybe even have a short holiday. Nothing exotic, but possibly a couple of weeks on one of the Costas.

He opened the door to Brian Jenkins book shop and was surprised at the tinkle of the old fashioned bell on the door. The shop was everything he had expected, something between a library and an antique shop. There was a subtle hint of must in the air, emanating obviously from the shelf upon shelf of old books. Books of every size and description and behind the counter Brian Jenkins peered benignly at him from behind the half moon glasses on the end of his nose. "Morning" he said amiably as Geraint approached him. "How can I help you?"

This was it, he was about to find out if his book was junk or treasure.

He placed the book on the counter and pushed it slowly towards the bookshop owner. "I just wondered if it might be worth something. I thought you could tell me, and perhaps make a deal?"

Brian Jenkins looked down at it for a moment or two then picked it up to study it closely. Suddenly, his demeanour changed and he dropped the book onto the counter. "I'm sorry. I can't help you. I have no customers for it."

Geraint thought quickly. Perhaps the old boy was

playing him, trying to get the book at a good price. "You haven't even looked at it properly, inside."

Brian Jenkins was white. "I have no wish to open it. As I said, I'm sorry but I can't help you with it."

Geraint looked at him from under a creased forehead. "But it's old, I know it's old and it looks kind of rare to me. Take another look. Please."

"I don't even want it in my shop. I'm sorry. Please take it away." He turned away from Geraint busying himself with a shelf of books behind him.

Geraint didn't move. He was watching his dreams of even a mediocre windfall drift away on a cloud of disappointment.

Brian Jenkins turned back to him. "You could try Solomon's Mines, the other end of the High Street. He turned and walked to the back of the shop leaving Geraint only one place to go. Out with his book.

Brian watched him move away from his shop front and immediately grabbed his telephone. He dialled the number in haste and had to redial it more slowly. It rang for what seemed like an age and then an old voice answered

"Hello?"

"It's me," he said quickly. "It was here. What we've been waiting for. No. Of course I didn't handle it, I'm not that stupid. No. I sent him to Solomon's Mines. No. It's closed today. I thought it would give us some time. Who? Oh, short, fat, glasses. Okay. Later."

He replaced the receiver in the old fashioned black Bakelite telephone that whirred when he turned the rotary dial and it rang with the sound of its original bells. He hesitated momentarily and then walked to the door and dropped the lock, then turned over the closed sign and turned off the lights. He couldn't clear his head and wanted to think straight and he wanted fresh air to rid himself of the pervading sense of being violated.

Geraint walked slowly back to his car and shoved the book firmly under the seat. Couldn't be too careful. Some people would pinch anything, even a worthless old book. He turned back towards the High Street and began walking purposefully down its length. He would be canny this time and not show his hand straight away, or the book. He could maybe make a few quid or two if he played it right.

He felt his spirits lift slightly, Old man Jenkins might not know a deal when he saw it but maybe this guy ... The shutters were down over the huge plate glass window and the sign on the door announced that Solomon's Mines was closed on a Thursday. Bugger it. He stood staring at the door as if it would open by the utterance of magical words then silently shook his head and started back towards his car. His feet heavier by each step. Oh well, he'd come back again tomorrow.

The short drive out of Monmouth did nothing to improve his mood and when he pulled up at the front of the Black Mountain Inn, his heart sank. Ruby's bicycle was propped against the wall.

He hesitated, then sighed, what was the matter with him? Ruby was a woman of the world, and she'd soon forget the whole incident. He pushed open the inn door.

Ruby was sitting on an old sofa by the fireplace; she obviously hadn't left after all. Must have been in the ladies when he had come back for the book. The book that was still under his car seat.

"Oh, Hi Ruby. Back in a minute." He dived out of the door and yanked open his car door, lunging under the seat to retrieve his still possible treasure.

His jacket was on the back seat and he pulled it to him, folding it carefully over the book, trying to appear casual under Ruby's sharp eyes.

Inside, he made for the stairs, "Just hang my jacket up, you couldn't put the kettle on by any chance. I could murder a cuppa."

He waited until she unfolded her bare legs, the short skirt rising to reveal more thigh that he wanted to see, then in the space of a heartbeat, found himself thinking about how good those thighs would feel wrapped around him. He put his jacket down on the bar, careful to keep the book concealed.

"Really, Ger? You really want tea? I think I can do better than that." She got up from the sofa in a way that suggested she had intended to look sexy, but she'd missed it by a couple of decades. But Geraint didn't see that, all he saw was Ruby, slowly unbuttoning her blouse and coming towards him.

What had he been thinking? This was Ruby, well known for her generosity in the bedroom department. Why not? It had been a long time.

He threw the bolt on the door and grabbed her none too gently, but she didn't protest, just laughed loudly. Encouraging him and taunting him at the same time.

He pushed her roughly back onto the sofa and was on top of her ripping off her blouse before he knew what he was doing. His kisses were rough and all of a sudden he felt angry and drew his hand back as if to slap her when it seemed as if he was suddenly released from a waking nightmare. He fell off her and ended up kneeling on the floor, head on his hands at the edge of the sofa.

Ruby was quiet as she stood up and straightened her skirt, silently buttoning her blouse. She said nothing as she went into the kitchen and switched on the kettle. There was a stray tear in the corner of her eye as the sound of the boiling water did nothing to drown Geraint's sobbing.

CHAPTER FOURTEEN: OLD BOOKS

Mike's first walk around was uneventful as he placed his equipment strategically around the building. His first impressions were of a spiritually quiet building but there were definite responses in him in certain locations. He found himself shivering on the galleried landing as he walked through what he thought to be a 'cold spot'. He flicked the switch on his voice recorder to make his first notes of the day.

"Mike Travis, April Twentieth, Two Thousand and Twelve. St. Winifride's Abbey, the Galleried Landing. Approximately half way along the landing there is a definite cold spot. Will return with thermal imaging camera, EVP recorder and check for physical drafts or other causes. No previous sighted phenomena recorded in this location." He clicked the machine off but remained still, developing his first impression before retracing his steps to the staircase.

At the head of the stairs he clicked on his voice recorder again.

"Main staircase. Previous sighted phenomena have been witnessed in this location. Has become known to residents and locals as the Blue lady. Thought to be Eleanor De Montefort. Static video camera, still camera and EVP in position."

He continued passing from room to room, repeating the preliminary procedures until he was happy that he'd covered every angle, and then sauntered into the kitchen in search of coffee.

He stopped abruptly just inside. Mary stood opposite, the startled rabbit look still very much in evidence but besmirched by lurid blue and black smudges around her eyes and inexpertly applied red lipstick that gave the impression of a deep gash where her lips should be. Her face was covered in a dark tan make-up that ended in a jagged line just beneath her chin. His heart went out her.

"Mary! I thought everyone had left. There isn't supposed to be any staff here during the investigation, in case it causes confusion with noises and such like. Er … are you going somewhere special?"

Mary flushed under the thick make-up that made her look like a clown from the Rocky Horror Show. "I'm a good girl. I am."

Mike nodded at her as he nonchalantly switched on the kettle, "I know you are. Where are you going?"

She shuffled around, staring down at her feet. "Nowhere."

"You're wearing a lot of make-up for nowhere."

More shuffling, then in almost a whisper, "I'm going to see my boyfriend."

Mike spooned instant coffee into a mug and poured boiling water into it. He said nothing as he reached into the small refrigerator for milk, giving her space to amplify the statement. She didn't.

He stirred sugar into his coffee noisily, smiling at her over the mug. "Boyfriend eh? Who is the lucky guy?"

He knew he'd pushed it too far as Mary swapped her startled rabbit look for belligerence. "It's none of your business. I'm a good girl."

Mike frowned. "I'm sorry. I didn't mean to be nosy, it's just that ."

"You didn't think I could get a boyfriend. No one thinks I can get a boyfriend. But I have," she said defiantly, thrusting out her chin.

He trod carefully. "Of course you can get a boyfriend; you're a very sweet girl. You're a good girl. It's just that you have such a sweet face, I wondered why you wanted to hide it with all that make-up."

She remained expressionless for several moments then

to his horror, she screwed up her face and dissolved into tears. "I … huh … knew it. I've made … a … huh mess of it." Her hands flew to her face.

Mike put the coffee mug down hastily, slopping coffee over the work surface and burning his fingers. He put his arm around her shoulder. "No, Mary! Hey, stop crying, please. I didn't mean to make you cry." He felt like a heel. She was right; it was none of his business. But … but he had an irrational need to protect the girl.

Mary turned into him, burying her head into his shoulder while she carried on crying. He was suddenly aware of the precarious nature of his situation, a situation he'd created himself. He released her gently and took a step back from her and then rested his hand on her arm.

"Please stop crying. Look, you've made your make-up run."

He turned to the sink and ripped a length of kitchen roll then wetted it under the tap. He turned back to her and began to gently clean the mess from her face.

"There you go, you look so much prettier now. You really don't need all that stuff. I think your boyfriend will much prefer you this way."

Mary was sniffing dejectedly.

"But he said … he said he wanted me to wear it. Like the other stuff."

Mike sensed something coming next that he really didn't want to hear.

"Mary, you don't need to tell me all about it. You were right; it's none of my business."

She sniffed. "He said if I loved him I would do all the other stuff. I'm a good girl," she said as if to herself.

"Mary look, maybe I'm not the best person to talk to, maybe your Mum?"

She shook her head. "She left when I was five."

"Do you have any sisters? Or an aunt?"

"No."

"Look, how about we have a cup of coffee and maybe

81

we can work something out. You really shouldn't let him make you do anything that you don't want to, you know."

She turned on him, runny eyes blazing. "You don't understand. I love him. I do. Maybe if I do that stuff he'll want to marry me. You should. You should mind your own business." She pushed passed him into the hallway.

He followed her. "Mary, wait. Look, come and sit down a minute. Tell me about your boyfriend. Please."

She hesitated.

"Let's have a coffee and you can tell me all about him. He's very lucky to have you for a girlfriend, I hope he knows that."

She seemed slightly mollified. "He's a very important man. He told me that I should be glad he picked me. He said I would look better with make-up and said I'd soon learn what to do. You know …"

Intense anger at the bastard that had, or intended to, defile the innocent blended seamlessly with compassion for her and the realisation that he was way out of his depth.

"You know what, Mary. You'd love my wife. Her name's Beth and she'd love to help you with the make-up thing. It's hard you know, to get it right. She does it very well and she's great at giving advice. Why don't I fix it for you to go and have tea or something? She'd love to meet you and she's so much better than me at the boyfriend thing. How about it?"

Mary nodded reluctantly. "I s'pose."

Mike was relieved. He decided to push his luck.

"What did you say his name was?"

She looked at her feet. "He said I wasn't supposed to say."

I bet he did.

He said, "Oh, I see, it's a secret."

She smiled and nodded. "Yes, it's a secret."

"How long have you known him, Mary? I mean it must be hard to keep such a special secret for so long."

She shook her head animatedly, "No, not really, I only met him a few days ago, so it's been easy."

Mike's heart sank.

"Mary, I know you don't know me, but I want you to trust me about something. Do you think you can do that?"

Mary looked thoughtful, then said in her breathless way, "Yes, because you've been on the telly."

For God's sake!

He decided not to pursue the premise that appearing on the television was the best in character references but weighing up the pros and cons decided it would be forgivable in the circumstances to play on her belief.

"Right. Well, Mary, I want you to go home. Don't go and meet him, he'll be all the more pleased to see you when you do." He took out one of his business cards and wrote a number on it, "That's my wife's telephone number and I want you to call her. Her name is Beth. Remember?"

Mary took it slowly. "But he'll be mad if I don't go to him."

"Maybe I can go and see him and tell him you had to go home because you were feeling unwell. He won't get mad then."

The frightened rabbit returned and she sprang to her feet and made for the door. She was gone before he could reach her.

Damn. He didn't have the luxury of being able to follow her and continue his persuasion, not with the investigation already under way. He pushed his hand through his prematurely grey hair, frustrated and more than concerned for the innocent. He had to just hope she's do as he'd asked her. For the moment, he had to continue with his investigation.

He picked up his infrared thermometer which detected and registered sudden or extreme temperature changes and the EMF Meter ready to sweep the building checking areas of electromagnetic energy, particularly the lower frequencies which had become acknowledged as possible indications of a spiritual energy. His scaled map in hand and pen stuck behind his ear, he began walking slowly throughout the ground floor rooms, limping badly as he had twisted his leg when he had tried to catch up with Mary. He began noting on the map the location of all readings received and their reference to mundane sources, such as electrical sockets, appliances and known wiring. The baseline readings were essential for him to have data to compare any activity during his investigation.

A glance at his watch showed eleven thirty and sightings of the Blue lady, or Eleanor, if indeed it was she that haunted the staircase, were reported between noon and twelve thirty. He headed for the landing at the top of the staircase where he had sensed a cold spot. His thermometer showed a significant drop in temperature. The surrounding areas read out at twenty degrees centigrade but as he stepped forward the digital readout quickly changed to ten degrees. He stood for a moment allowing the thermometer to settle then very slowly stepped forwards one pace at a time until the readout shot up again to twenty degrees. He stepped back to the location of the original reading and repeated the process in a three sixty degree arc. Finally satisfied that he'd pinpointed the centre of the cold spot he marked the map with a blue X. Then putting his equipment on a half moon table against the wall he began searching for the source of the cold draft.

The wall of the corridor wasn't cold to the touch and a thorough examination showed no openings or drafts coming from any of the doorways nor were there any windows. The ceiling was high but there were no visible openings, the glass dome being completely sealed and temperature directly below it was at twenty. Air from the ground floor was twenty degrees and so he concluded that there were no obvious physical reasons for the thermal drop.

His initial EMF reading was around five milligauss

which indicated a possible source of spirit energy. The surrounding area was significantly higher and within what was considered normal range.

Mike pulled out his voice recorder. "Mike Travis, Galleried landing. Initial impression of a cold spot was born out by infrared thermometer recording a temperature drop of ten degrees. EMF showed extremely low frequency of five. Area has been marked on map. Continuing."

He moved onwards along the landing to a heavy oak framed door. To the side of the door was a notice; DANGER. Unsafe masonry and timbers. ENTRY PROHIBITED. There was a massive bolt and padlock reinforcing the idea.

He turned around and retraced his steps back to the staircase, noting the temperature drop and low frequency as he passed back through the cold spot.

At the top of the stairs he stopped. The hairs on the back of his neck and his arms were at attention and he shivered. He spun around. There was nothing to see.

He leaned in to the thermal imaging video camera positioned at the stair head and switched it on. He did likewise to his voice recorder. Lowering his own voice, he said into it, "Electronic Voice Phenomena recording, main staircase… Hello?" He paused and listened. There was nothing. "Hello, my name is Mike, is there a spirit presence here?" He paused again. "Eleanor de Montefort, are you here?" Again there was nothing but the cold spot seemed to expand and fill the entire area; his thermometer now reading ten degrees along the entire landing. There was movement in the air and he stood still allowing it to pass over him. His EMF meter was a symphony of dancing lights and the readings were fluctuating wildly.

A blue grey shadow appeared at the head of the stairwell and slowly moved down their length to the hallway below.

"Well, I'll be damned," he muttered.

Following the shadow which now had taken on the rough outline of a person, he entered the drawing room. There was a cold chill in the room which had been comfortable earlier. He took readings from his thermometer and the EMF meter and noted them carefully on the map.

"Continuing EVP session, now in drawing room on the ground floor. Hello. I'm Mike and I would like to communicate with you if you are able. Can you let me know you are there in some way?" His EMF meter lights picked up their dance routine again and as he turned to scan the room, a feather light touch on his cheek brought him to a halt. His EMF meter returned to its steady green light and he could physically feel the rise in temperature around him. He hoped the video camera had caught something tangible worth documentation because if there had been a spirit presence, it had now gone. He checked his watch, it was twelve fifteen. Before leaving the room he checked once more that the video recorder was still rolling and placed his voice recorder next to it, switched on.

Mike left the drawing room and repeated the process from room to room with spare equipment with no result. He returned to the library to begin his initial draft report. He'd learned early on not to get excited when something happened in the way it had there. Emotions out of control had no place in a serous investigation. He expected a quiet time from then until around ten o'clock when reports of loud knocking and footsteps had been heard in the hallway. It was already four o'clock and he had time to do more research. He planned to stay in the library and read the book that Radford had left on the desk entitled *St.Winifride's Abbey: A History*.

Eleanor De Montefort featured prominently in the period between 1640 and 1654 when she had died, apparently in childbirth. And there was a brief paragraph stating that her husband had fallen foul of the locals when rumours had spread that he was involved in the black arts and had been witnessed conjuring demons.

He raised his eyebrows, this was new. Unfortunately the author had not expanded on the theme.

He pondered momentarily then stood up suddenly and crossed to the bank of mahogany bookshelves filled with leather bound volumes of varying age. Scanning shelf after shelf he finally came upon a line of ten matching volumes entitled A History of Monmouthshire by Sir Joseph Bradney. A glance inside the first volume informed him that the entire works spanned the sixteenth to the twentieth centuries. Trial and error brought him to the seventeenth century. He took it back to the large Queen Anne chair by the fireplace and settled down to read.

CHAPTER FIFTEEN: WET BARE FOOTPRINTS

Kath Dickinson, the midwife, sat in an armchair facing the window, sipping her tea.

"You have found yourself a beautiful home Beth."

"Yes. We fell in love with it as soon as we saw it. There's a lot of work to do in the garden but I've got a picture of it in my mind. How it's going to be; full of fragrant herbs and flowers, especially lavender. It's going to be a beautiful garden for this one to grow up in and play in." She rested her hand on her belly.

"Well, on that subject, let's talk baby. I know you haven't registered with our GP yet. I can see what you're up against," she nodded at the boxes. "But this late in your pregnancy you should be getting regular check up from the doctor. No worries, I can do that for you, you just pop into the surgery and sign the forms when you've got your breath back. I assume you've been having regular ante natal checks before you moved here?"

"Yes, every month."

"Well, you should be getting checked more often at this stage. Let's discuss the birth for a minute. Have you heard of the domino birth system?"

Beth shook her head.

"It's one of the new ways of thinking," said Kath, "and it's a lovely way to give birth. As this is your first we don't recommend a home birth, especially as we're a long way from the local maternity unit, but a domino birth is the next best thing. You see the same midwife all the way through, that would be me," she beamed. "I visit you on a weekly basis from here on in as you're close to term and when your labour starts you call me and I come straight to

89

you and stay here with you, then when your labour progresses I take you to the maternity unit and stay with you throughout the birth. Then, if everything is okay, you can come home a few hours later. It means you can stay in your own home a lot longer, and your husband can be with you throughout."

Beth was smiling. "That sounds lovely."

Kath beamed back at her. "Any notions about water births or any other alternative? Right then, let's have a look at you and start all the paperwork. I don't suppose you have your previous ante natal records handy?"

"Actually, yes. I'll go and get them. Would you like some more tea?"

Kath shook her head, "No, thanks. I only popped round on the off chance of catching you; I'm due to see Joan Davis in half an hour. Twins this time!"

Beth heaved herself from the sofa and padded out into the dining room to retrieve her records from her old writing desk. When she returned, Kath was standing at the window. A sudden pain in Beth's temple made her stop and rub the side of her head. She looked out of the window.

She was there. Standing at the bridge. She glanced quickly at Kath who gave no indication that she could see the woman.

"Here they are," Beth said quickly.

"Are you okay? You look pale."

"I'm fine, I just got up too quickly I expect."

"Well sit back down and let me look at you. Pop your feet up and let me listen to that little one of yours." She took the conical stethoscope from her bag. "This is a pinard, to let me hear your baby's heartbeat. You must have had this done a hundred times by now."

Beth nodded enthusiastically as she lay down on the sofa and bared her belly for the midwife.

Kath leaned in, ear against the end of the pinard and pressed it against Beth. She listened intently for a few moments and then took it away with a flourish. "Everything seems fine. Now let's have a look at your blood pressure."

Beth covered her belly and took her arm out of her sleeve.

Kath wrapped the cuff around her arm and pressed the switch to inflate it, watching the digital readout closely. The cuff seemed to inflate forever and became quite painful.

Eventually, Kath released the pressure, frowning. "Hm. Your blood pressure is quite high. I expect you've overdone it with the move."

Beth was about to protest when Kath turned back to her bag. She smiled reassuringly at her. "It's not dangerously high at the moment but it's much higher than I'd like. Do you mind if I make a quick check with the doc?"

Beth frowned, she'd been overdoing it. "No," she murmured, "Go ahead."

Kath took her phone from her leather case and dialled, smiling and nodding reassurance at Beth.

"It's probably just the move, I just want to …Hi, it's Kath. Is Doc Graham there? Cheers." She was silent for a moment. "Doctor Graham, it's Kath Dickinson. Yes fine thanks. I wanted to have a quick chat about a new patient. Just moved into the area coming to the end of the third trimester… eight months … Yes. Look, I'm not too concerned but her blood pressure is quite high, could be the stress of the move and may settle. What do you want me to do? … Okay, will do. And you'll leave me a script to cover it? Fine. Thanks Doctor Graham. Yes, and you. Bye."

She smiled reassurance at Beth. "Doc says he wants you to take some medication to control your blood pressure. It can be dangerous if it goes unchecked at this stage. Just for a couple of days and I'll come and check it again, see how you're doing. All right?"

She dived back into her leather case and produced a small brown bottle of tablets. I want you to take one of these at night. They should do the trick. "

Beth frowned. "Are you sure? I'm sorry, I mean ... I'd rather not take any pills unless I have to. Maybe if I rest up?"

"High blood pressure is far more dangerous if it's left untreated Beth, especially during pregnancy and especially in the later stages. Doc Graham wouldn't have prescribed them otherwise. I'll call into the surgery on my way back and get the doc to write the prescription up for you. In the meantime I'd like you to take one now. I'll get you some water." She was in the kitchen before Beth could pull herself up.

"The glasses are in the cupboard on the left," she called out.

"Found them! So, where did you move from? Oh yes, I have the name of your previous doctor on your old records; I'll do the registration for you, save you the hassle. You should really rest up, you know. I want to see that blood pressure improved when I come back. I think I'll make the visits twice weekly, I want to keep an eye on you."

Beth looked worried. "Is it that serious? I mean, I feel fine."

Kath returned with the water. "It's purely precautionary. It's your first baby and you've just moved house and don't know anyone yet. It's a response to stress I expect. I just want to make sure everything settles down before the big day. So, did you ask the sex of the wee one when you had your scan?"

Beth shook her head as she swallowed the tablet.

"Don't want to know? Some of my mums don't want to know, some do." She said happily.

Beth smiled knowingly, "I'm certain it's a girl."

"I hope you won't be disappointed then. Have you thought of names yet?"

"No, we decided to wait and meet her first. We'll know the name that suits her when we see her for the first time."

Kath laughed. "You really are sure it's a girl. Well, you won't have long to wait. About a week I'd say."

Beth sat up too quickly. "A week? I've a month to go yet."

Kath shook her head, "Not in my book. Baby's head is well engaged and ready for action. Maybe you had your dates wrong?"

"But the scan?"

"Scans tell us a lot, but they can't account for nature. Babies come when their ready, not before and not after." She put a reassuring hand on Beth's arm. "You'll be fine. I'll pop back the day after tomorrow and I want to see you rested, madam, and hopefully with a lower blood pressure."

She busied herself with her notes then stood abruptly. "You stay there and rest, I'll see myself out. Get your husband to do the cooking and the washing up, it's an order! In the meantime, if you have any concerns, no matter how small, call me. I left my number next to the kettle." She beamed at Beth as she let herself out through the kitchen door.

Beth put her hand on her forehead as she lay back against the pillows. A week! And high blood pressure. She wanted Mike.

She looked over at her phone; she knew he would have his on silent during his investigation. He normally had it switched off, but since they knew she was pregnant it was never off when he was away from her. She picked it up and dialled his number; it rang and then went to his voicemail. Then, not wanting to scare him she just left the message, "Hi, it's me, just missing you. See you in the morning. Love you."

She settled back against the cushions and closed her eyes.

The rhythmic whirring sound with its regular clicks

came again. She opened her eyes wide and struggled to sit up. What *was* that?

She listened intently then closed her eyes again, listening without visual input may help pinpoint the source. Somewhere in her head there was the lilt of an old nursery tale. *Rapunzel, Rapunzel, let down your hair.*

Beth let herself drift, suddenly tired, into the story. The girl in the tower with her spinning wheel.

Spinning wheel! That was the sound she was hearing. She'd heard it before in a working museum. The sound coming from the alcove near the fireplace was the sound made by a spinning wheel.

She shook her head, unable to make sense of it and then also unable to keep her eyes open, she allowed herself to float back into a pleasurable sleep.

The light was fading and she was hungry, and her baby was kicking her just under her diaphragm when she woke. Unsure if it was the latter or the sound that woke her, she propped herself up on her elbow and listened.

There it was again, a sort of wet slapping sound. It seemed to be coming from the kitchen. Alarmed in case Kath had left the tap running when she had brought her the water she pushed herself upright and stood up, arching her back before stepping lively into the kitchen. Her eyes went first to the sink. The tap wasn't running, then casting around she could see nothing that would have caused the noise.

As she turned to put the kettle on, she stopped dead. The red quarry tiles on the kitchen floor were covered in wet footprints. Bare wet footprints.

CHAPTER SIXTEEN: THE JOURNAL

Sir John Bradney had done his job well except for the lean information regarding Eleanor De Montefort. It appeared that other readers had felt the same as there were jottings in the margins of the page, written small and close together in pencil. The words had smudged slightly and faded, so Mike moved over to the desk and held the book directly under the ornate lamp.

After a moment of squinting at the handwriting he read, *De Montefort's Journal 1654. Eleanor's death is not the end.*

De Montefort's Journal. Gavin Radford hadn't given that one away. He wondered if the journal still existed and if so, was it there?

He limped back across the room to the bookshelves and began a fingertip search of the titles. Was it likely that the old journal, even if it still existed would be among the other books? He hoped so.

An hour passed as he painstakingly examined every book within his reach and then reluctantly pulled the library steps over to the beginning of the shelves to examine the higher volumes. If the journal was there, he was going to find it.

He saw immediately that the nature of the volumes on the high shelf were all treatises on the occult. Most of them appeared of a great age and were obvious collector's items, some were spurious later copies made for mass distribution under the guise of being original works on the black art.

Mike let out a whistle. The collection wasn't priceless but to the right person it was extremely valuable. If nothing else, it showed that at some time, the owner of the library was into some heavy dark stuff.

He took the first volume down. The Necromicon.

It was widely acknowledged that the majority of the versions of the book were for the most part works of fiction based on the books of Lovecraft. All except one, known as the Simon Necronomicon.

And this was it.

Mike knew he held a few grand's worth of book. In its day, the book was considered so dangerous that it could destroy a man's life if used without caution or protection, or if it were played with carelessly for thrills, such as often happened in the Victorian era and way back, as men strove to find wealth any way they could.

He understood enough to put it back on the shelf unopened.

The next volume appeared even older and its pages were brittle and fragile. The Clavicule of Solomon, or the Key of Solomon as it was now known, was basically a book on demonology, commonplace in any decent library, though God alone knew why. He'd seen the book before whilst researching a case. It hadn't made for bedtime reading but for the most part it was widely replicated and easily downloaded from the good old internet. It was the antiquity of the volume that made it a wealthy collector's piece. There were several versions of the Key of Solomon in existence, translated into various languages. It was believed that there was no copy earlier than a latin text from the fourteenth century. This one was a copy dated 1603.

Run of the mill volumes by Arthur Edward Waite were adjacent, although there was nothing of any major significance. These were followed by copies of the Malleus Maleficarum, known as the Hammer of the Witches, a text that dealt with methods of how to identify and punish witches and a copy of The Discoverie of Witches, a similar tome.

Next to them was a leather bound book of obvious age but it had no title. Mike's heart rate picked up its pace. He took the book down carefully. No inscriptions appeared anywhere on the outside. It was held closed by a leather thong threaded through the old cover, worn thin over the years from fastening and unfastening.

He tugged on it gently and the cover fell open. On the first page in faded ink and in a scrawling, generous hand was inscribed, *Hugo De Montefort. His Journal, the year of our Lord 1653 unto May 1654.*

Bingo! Mike descended the steps slowly, the pain in his leg had reached a crescendo and he knew he would have to give in and take more pain killers. He didn't want to as any reference to him taking strong pain killing drugs could make his findings appear unsound. But he knew when he was beaten. He unscrewed the cap on the small brown bottle and tossed two Tramadol into his mouth and swallowed hard. It was going to be a long evening.

He put the book onto the table at the side of the Queen Ann chair then headed for the kitchen. More caffeine was definitely in order. It would speed the effect of the Tramadol and sharpen his focus. Above all he needed to be objective. The scribblings of the guy from the seventeenth century may have nothing whatsoever to do with his investigation. Or maybe they did.

He half expected to see Mary in the kitchen and he frowned as his concern once again focussed on the unfortunate young girl. As soon as the investigation was complete he would have a word with Gavin. He was the manager of the trust after all and as such had responsibility to a certain extent for his staff, especially one who was clearly challenged in intellect. Maybe the inimitable Mrs. Evans would take her under her wing. He shook his head at the realisation that those wings were not made for taking stray chicks under.

He made the instant coffee and wrinkled his nose. Beth made wonderful coffee; this was clearly the cheapest around and was bitter and acrid. He smiled at the thought of Beth, snuggled up on the sofa, she'd better be! And their new home, full of promise and the prospect of their first child not too far away. He was indeed, to quote Jack, a lucky bastard.

Settling back into the chair and feeling a chill, he wished the fire in the hearth had been alight, but comfort wasn't the object of this exercise. The acrid coffee went down slowly, as Mike poured over the journal.

The early entries were mostly of a domestic nature. Complaints about slovenly staff, an attempt at some basic accounting. And then on the thirtieth of the September of 1653 the tone changed dramatically.

I can scarce believe it. The work I hath proclaimed in the name of the Daemon hath rewarded me. My dearest Eleanor is with childe. Zillah hath told to me that it will be born in the month of May. Astaroth hath indeed been generous unto me. I thank the stars for the daye I made the acquaintance of him at the Assizes.

The next pages were filled with praise for him, whoever he was, and for Astaroth who it seemed was the source of the generosity. And from the following entries, the 'he' of the journal was obviously a regular guest at the Abbey. There were many paragraphs devoted to Eleanor as she grew daily with the child she carried.

The tone changed suddenly and 'he', seemed suddenly out of favour.

The entry on April the twenty fifth bore witness.

I am afeared of him. He that proclaimeth death on those before him for trafficke with the Devil and him in league with the daemons of the pit. I hath wrought such sins that my soul be surely blackened. Howe shall I speak of these things to Eleanor? I hath taken the treasure and hath secreted it within these walls where he shall not find it nor defile it.

Then on the twenty ninth of April 1654

Her screams can be heard throughout the house and the servants are quiet and gathered in the chapel. All except old Zillah who is with her in her bedchamber. In God's name what have I brought us to?

April Thirtieth 1654

Everything that I afeared hath come to pass. Eleanor is dead. My beautiful Eleanor, what hath I wrought? The childe is alive but frail. A girl childe. Zillah has gone to seek out a wet nurse. I can hardly bear to hear the mewling of the weakling infant but I must do what must be done. For Eleanor.

He is coming. He is coming for the childe. I am taking her to the chapel and I will baptise her myself in the name of God and ask for forgiveness and that he heap not the sins of this father onto the innocent head of our daughter. It is all the protection I can give her. I shall name her Marie Katherine according to wishes of my dearest Eleanor. I pray he daresn't enter for fear of the wrath of God. I fear God's wrath not, for whatever befalleth me now is of my own creation. God have mercy on my soul.

Astaroth's generosity, it seemed, had come with a price. It continued,

Zillah hath taken the childe to a place of safety. I hath committed the unforgivable sin and hath taken a life. In pretence of going forthe to deliver the childe unto him, I ventured to the Assizes and in a secret place I ran him through and buried his abominable remains. His filthy book shall never see the light of daye and is interred upon his breast. I cower in fear of the night when the Daemon will return to claim the childe as his own. I shall not live another daye.

Mike flicked back to the inside cover to check the dates. Hugo had been correct in his assumption.

What did it all mean? And did it have any bearing on the investigation? If the reports of the Blue Lady were accurate and it was indeed the restless spirit of Eleanor De Montefort, then apparently she had good reason for the restlessness. A big 'if'.

He'd seen the shadow figure on the staircase and documented the cold spot on the galleried landing, but there was no proof without concrete evidence.

He decided to retrieve the voice recorder and run it through the software on the laptop. One could live in hope.

As he crossed the hallway a cold draft blew across his face. Nothing unusual in such an old building. He carried on towards the drawing room. Until he felt a hand on his arm.

O-kay.

"Hello. Is that Eleanor De Montefort? I'm here to listen to you if you can communicate in any way." He paused. "Eleanor?"

The cold breeze ruffled through his hair. He grabbed the EMF meter from his pocket and the lights were doing their frantic dance all over the screen whilst the digital readout was fluctuating from one to five and back again.

As quickly as it had appeared, the cold draft disappeared, and the hairs on his arms settled down again. He made for the drawing room, retrieved the voice recorder and returned to the library where he immediately connected the recorder to his laptop and initiated the software that would seek out and analyse any electronic voice phenomena that was below the frequency of human hearing, but if captured, would play back.

He heard his own voice say, "Hello. I'm Mike and I would like to communicate with you if you are able. Can you let me know you are there in some way?" His voice was accompanied by the static sound of white noise, another good sign.

The white noise continued for a few seconds and then he took a step back, almost falling over the chair. The voice was low but distinct. It was a woman's voice.

"He is coming ... He is coming for the childe ... Protect the childe."

Mike was visibly shaken. He'd heard voices from EVP sessions before, but had kept an open mind as some of the recorded voices were ambiguous to say the least. This voice, however, was not.

"Fucking hell!" he exclaimed, and then as if in deference to the lady, "Sorry, Eleanor, but that was awesome."

He played it again.

And again.

"He is coming ... He is coming for the childe ... Protect the childe."

CHAPTER SEVENTEEN: THE WOMAN AT THE BRIDGE

Beth stood as if turned to stone. The wet footprints began at the back door

The back door that was still closed.

They carried on up to the door of her dining room and ended abruptly in a large puddle. As she stood staring at the floor, her heart lurched as the footprints and puddle dried up as she stared at them, and were gone in a heartbeat.

She felt decidedly unsteady and held on to the doorframe until she regained her balance. Suddenly, everything fell into place. The pain in her temple that occurred only when the woman in the garden appeared. The woman standing by the bridge. The spinning wheel and now the footprints. They were clearly not alone in their new home.

She hurried through the dining room into the living room and grabbed her phone, pressing the button to redial her last call. She needed Mike. To speak to him at least, to ask him not to waste time at the abbey, she needed him.

The call went through to his voicemail. She hesitated and then said, "It's me Mike. Look, something's happened here. Don't worry, I'm fine. It's the woman again. And the bridge. The bridge from my dream. Oh no, you don't know about that yet. And now there's wet footprints in the kitchen, and … and I need you."

After she had left the message, she immediately regretted it. She knew his reaction would be to abandon the investigation and return home immediately he heard the recording. She felt guilty. She'd over reacted. She redialled and waited for his voice telling her to leave a

103

message.

"Mike, it's me. Look, I'm fine. Ignore the last message; I'll explain when you come home in the morning. Love you."

She relaxed a little and went to sit down on the sofa, then mindful of the midwife's warning, she put her feet up and lay back on the cushions to think about what had happened.

Mike hadn't seen the woman, but that didn't mean she wasn't there. He didn't see every spirit or ghost. And she remembered the sensation when she had first seen Fenn Dawson in Crowsmoor, it was the same feeling. Now the footprints. She needed to make sense of it.

She thought about the midwife and the high blood pressure. Maybe she was right. Maybe she had overdone things with the move. High blood pressure would explain the headaches. Maybe she was overtired and making more of things than were actually there.

But the footprints had been real. At least for a minute or two before they disappeared. Including the puddle.

Beth felt uneasy again and cast a glance over her shoulder into the kitchen and back out of the window. There was no woman and no footprints on the kitchen floor.

She got up again after several minutes, realising that she was still hungry. The fridge was particularly uninspiring until she spotted the bag of miniature chocolate bars. A few minutes later she had a plate of mini Mars bars, a packet of crisps and a hunk of cheese, and a glass of milk in her other hand. Healthy it was not, mouth-watering to her pregnant taste it definitely was. She stopped by the tall larder cupboard and added two pickled onions for good measure.

She laughed aloud as she pictured Mike's face when he saw her cravings translated onto a plate. Thought of him settled her nerves a little; he would make sense of it all in the morning no doubt.

The baby was doing the fandango on her bladder and she got up hastily. The room swam and she found herself falling backwards missing the edge of the sofa by inches and falling down hard onto the floor.

The wind left her forcibly and the nausea that swamped her made her retch. Instinctively, her hand flew to her stomach. The baby kicked out hard in protest.

She held her breath as the infant wriggled as much as it could in the now confined space of her womb. Her heart was racing and she was still holding her breath while the child continued its kicking protest.

Eventually she breathed again. There was no abdominal pain and the baby was moving.

"I'm so sorry, sweetheart. Please be all right."

She leaned onto the edge of the sofa and pushed herself up, then lay down to rest.

Not wanting to do any further thinking that day she flicked the switch on the TV remote and settled down to watch a third rerun of some mind numbing soap opera. Their satellite dish was still in the garage and they had no phone line as yet. But mind numbing was what she craved right then and so as the characters played out their various dramas she felt herself drifting back off to sleep.

Before she got there however, the TV suddenly changed to a different channel and she found herself watching the demise of a family of gorillas in the tropical rain forest. Then in the next instant she was thrown into the midst of a family quiz show. The TV kept flicking through its channels of its own volition.

"Okay. I get it. There's someone here. Well, just so you know, I'm not scared. So if you'd do me a favour and stop this, I'd be very grateful."

The TV returned to the everyday traumas of a northern family.

"Thanks," Beth said, her voice steeped in ice cubes. She wasn't in the mood for any more.

The TV switched itself off.

"All right. You win. I don't know who you are, but I'm tired and if you have something to tell me, stop doing it in riddles and dreams I don't understand. Come on. Speak up. Who are you?"

The whisper was barely audible, "….ain."

The silence that followed was deafening as Beth strained every sinew to try and hear something. Anything. It had gone very quiet.

She lay back on the cushions trying to keep her emotions in check, but the events of the day won the battle and she found herself crying into the sofa, gentle sobs muffled by the cushions.

She managed to pull herself together and sniffing, she wiped her eyes on the sleeve of her top, unable and unwilling to lift herself from the sofa one more time.

The sniffs eventually slowed and petered out. Her eyes stung and she felt incredibly weary and in moments she gave way to the inevitable. She fell into a fitful sleep.

She was there again. The woman at the bridge. And she was beckoning to her to follow. Beth followed without thinking. The woman didn't turn back once. Beth realised she was watching a replay of the dream she had had previously. In her sleep, she smiled. It was a happy dream. The woman was going to meet her husband, the charcoal burner, to give him the news of her pregnancy. They lay in the clearing and ate the food the woman had brought. She could almost taste the lemonade. She could feel the warmth of his body as he embraced her. His name was on her lips again. Owain.

But what of the woman? Her name still eluded her.

Then he spoke again, "I am full of joy, Adain, my wife. How blessed we are."

Adain. She heard the whisper again, '…ain'. So her name was Adain.

But what did she want of her?

CHAPTER EIGHTEEN: WITCHCRAFT

Brookstone 1654.

The civil war had come to Wales and Cromwell's army had marched on St. Fagan's and Owain had heard the news in the market square in Monmouth. The King was almost defeated and the loyalist army was diminished and all able bodied men were being taken into their ranks. He thanked God for his occupation; charcoal was in demand by both civilian nobility and the militia. It was unlikely that he would be plucked from Adain.

He decided not to pass the news on to her, not wanting her to have something other than their coming child to worry about. Times were difficult enough without the anxiety of him being dragged off to war, however unlikely.

He took his kerchief from around his neck and wiped away the sweat on his brow. Looking skyward he saw the sun at its zenith, she would be there soon, stepping lightly through the forest into the clearing. He wondered how long it would be before it was too far for her to come as her pregnancy drew on. She was fit and healthy but the burden of the child would make it impossible for her to walk the distance.

Moments later he heard her softly humming and she appeared at the edge of the clearing, basket over her arm.

He walked quickly to greet her, enfolding her in his muscular arms. He kissed her lightly on the top of her head.

"Adain. The hours I am from you are long indeed. How are you and the little one this day?"

She beamed at him and wiped a stray sooty smudge from his cheek.

"We are both well, husband. Do not afear yourself so."

He kissed her again and smiled in return.

They ate quietly in appreciation of the fine day and each other. It was time for her to leave all too soon, but he wanted her to return home to safety. There had been talk of King's men in the forest.

"My love, I hear there are soldiers in these parts. I want you to stay in our home until they have moved on. I will send word."

She looked thoughtful before she said, "I will do as you say, husband. Not because I am afeared of the soldiers but I wish not to cause you a troubled mind."

She stood on her toes and put her arms around his neck. "The others in the hamlet will tell me when they have gone. Then I will come again."

His face relaxed. He would miss her sorely but more than that he needed to know she was in the safety of their little cottage by the brook. They took their leave tenderly and she picked up her basket and walked slowly to the edge of the forest before turning and waving to him.

He watched the dark space where she had stood and with a heavy heart returned his attentions to the charcoal pit.

The breeze through the trees was warm on her face as she tried to hold back the tears of loneliness that she felt in her heart already. It was dusty on the path through the woods, despite the heavy carpet of pine needles, and she stopped briefly for another drink of lemonade from the stone jar in her basket.

She paused and looked around her, listening, breathing in the forest. Something was different.

The birds were silent and there were no scurrying sounds of small animals in the bracken. It was as if the forest was holding its breath.

Then in the distance the muffled thump of horses' hooves on the dry path drifted towards her on the warm breeze. Horses in the forest were foreign to her experience. She stood still, frowning, listening.

The steady thump of the hooves seemed to be coming closer and they also seemed to be approaching from different directions. She dropped the basket and the stone jar onto the carpet of pine needles and picked up the hem of her skirts, hurrying now for home.

In minutes she was running as the sound of the horses drew ever closer. Then without warning she caught her foot in a wandering root and fell headlong onto the path. Instinctively her hand flew to her belly. She was winded but otherwise unhurt but she threw her consciousness within, to the child, still so delicate.

There was no pain in her womb, so she stood again, wincing at pain that flamed through her ankle.

The horse and its rider were in front of her in an instant and her hands cupped her face in shock. The rider wore a dark velvet coat and a plume in his wide brimmed hat. He was without mistake a King's man.

In seconds two others joined him from the opposite direction. They steadied their horses and remained staring at her in silence. Then the first rider dismounted and patted the horse's flank. Removing the heavy leather gauntlets he approached her. His eyes glinted menace and lust and she found herself silently praying to the Goddess for protection.

"Well met, wench. Thou wilt provide us with a deal of entertainment this day, I'll warrant."

She stepped back away from him and he laughed loudly, bringing a smirk to the faces of his companions. "Where doth thou thinkest thou art bound?"

She didn't answer.

He stepped towards her and she turned to run. To run back to Owain. And as she did, another horseman appeared behind her. She was surrounded.

The fourth man dismounted. "Enough! There will be sport enough when she hath done what will be done for Sir Thomas. The task is to find her and take her thither."

He lunged at her and there was nowhere to run. He grabbed her roughly and pulled her arms behind her back sending shards of agony into her shoulders.

Pain brought defiance, and with it speech. "Where art thou taking me?" she demanded.

"Thou art the wench that abides beside the brook? And thou hast knowledge of the healing plants?"

Adain dropped her eyes; there was only one way that this was going. She was about to be accused of witchcraft.

"Thou hast been commanded to visit with Sir Thomas and apply thy healing arts."

There was no reason to trust the man but there was no choice and if the words he spoke were indeed the truth then perhaps Sir Thomas would spare her.

"What aileth him?"

Her question brought derisive laughter from the men. The grip tightened on her arms bringing fresh waves of pain. She gritted her teeth and closed her eyes against the tears that threatened to overwhelm her.

"Why naught but the pox!" the man said. "The physicians can do naught to cure him but it is said that thou taketh away the pox from one in a neighbouring village. Be that the truth?"

She knew that to deny it would bring about a fate worse than tending to the pox addled judge but to acknowledge it as truth would see her taken to the assizes as in league with the Devil. She decided to play for time.

She nodded. "It be the truth."

The man holding her yanked her painfully towards him, she could smell the sweat on his unwashed body and bit down on her lip to counteract the rising nausea and before she could protest she found herself lifted and thrown over the saddle of the horse. Its rider held her there while two of the others bound her with rope.

He jumped up behind her and turned the horse into the path out of the forest.

CHAPTER NINETEEN: ELEANOR

Mike's initial reaction gave way to fascination. It was the clearest evidence captured in this way that he had experienced. In conjunction with what he had just read, he was convinced that the spirit of Eleanor De Montefort was indeed still in residence at the Abbey.

He picked up the journal again and read the entry that spoke of Eleanor's death. The words leapt out at him. They were the exact words on the tape. 'He is coming. He is coming for the child. Protect the child.'

Turning the page he read the final entry. Hugo De Montefort had committed a murder and was in fear of his life. No further entries suggested that his fears had in fact been valid. Mike grabbed the History of Monmouthshire and flicked through it until he reached the brief entry regarding the abbey and searched for confirmation. Hugo De Montefort had indeed died on April 30th 1654. There was no mention as to the manner of his death.

Daylight was almost gone and he checked his watch, amazed at the passage of time. Further research would have to wait; his investigation was far from over.

Out in the hallway the light from the chandelier flickered. He moved quickly but on reaching the hall the light was steady.

Don't over react. It's an old building and you're letting your judgment be clouded by what you've just read. Classic mistake. Focus.

He stood in the centre of the hallway listening, scanning the area. There was no sound and nothing to see. He turned to go back into the library and then paused thoughtfully. The journal had made mention of a chapel. Well of course there had been a chapel; the place was an old abbey! No mention had been made of a chapel when he spoke to the staff and Gavin had said nothing. Of course. The crypt. Back in the days of persecution, chapels and other places of Catholic worship had been the focus of much violence against the clergy and were often hidden.

He had placed a camera down there next to the stone effigies and tombs, where better to capture any restless spirits than at their graveside? But there had been no reports of activity down there. He made for the stone staircase that lead to the crypt.

The bang came from above, swiftly followed by another and the sound of footsteps. Mike whirled around and took the stairs as quickly as his leg would allow him. At the top he stood listening. There were footsteps again. He turned in their direction; the sounds were coming from behind the padlocked door.

He moved as close to it as he could and took out his voice recorder, desperately hoping the sounds would be repeated and captured digitally. He spoke into the device.

"Mike Travis, galleried landing. EVP session at locked off door... Hello? Is someone there?"

The banging had changed to a muted knocking sound. He knocked on the door, three short knocks. There was no further sound. He took the padlock in his hand and looked sideways at the forbidding notice. The last thing he needed was to fall through rotting timbers. He remained on the landing for thirty minutes during which time he heard nothing else.

Back in the library he was unsettled. There were several hours before he was due to leave and he wanted to cast aside his own set of rules regarding an investigation and would allow himself further research. He could make arrangements with Gavin to return. The last thing he wanted was to make the evidence fit the history, they had to be handled separately and if they supported each other then he would have a case for paranormal events. A haunting.

He played the recorder back again, checking himself against preconception, but the voice remained as plain as ever through the crackle of the white noise. "He is coming. He is coming for the childe. Protect the childe."

Which child? Eleanor's baby? And who was 'he'?

He made the decision, he would return to finish the investigation and leave the equipment running in their various locations while he continued searching the library for more information.

The journal was the first place to start as he tried to piece together the story.

Hugo had said that the 'he' had condemned people for the crime of witchcraft whilst practicing the black arts privately. He would therefore be in a position of some authority and of high standing in the community. He had also been a regular guest at the abbey, confirming Mike's theory of being a prominent member of society. A priest maybe? A noble? No. To be in a position of being able to condemn a person to his death, he had to be a judge.

Mike reached out for The History of Monmouthshire again. Sir John Bradney was sure to have made mention of any prominent judges of the day.

The index sited several Justices scattered throughout the text. The first reference was early on in the fourth volume and related to the death of Eduard Bolling who was the local Justice in the town of Abergavenny. He was ninety three. The second reference was about a Sir Rufus Stanhope who had died in the Battle of Naseby during the Civil War.

Sir Thomas Llewellyn was next on the list. He began reading the sizeable entry.

After several minutes, Mike lowered the book onto the desk and sat back against the chair. Judge Thomas Llewellyn had earned himself a considerable reputation for his harsh judgements and cruel sentences. His main concern it seemed had been trying folk for witchcraft which bore a mandatory death sentence and many had been condemned without trial. His methods of exacting a confession were guaranteed the result he wanted. Torture took the place of a fair trial. He regularly sat in judgement at Assizes held in The Black Mountain Inn where he oversaw the carrying out of the death sentences he had ordered. Prisoners were hung from the high beam above the stairwell. He was as famous for the rabid obsession with the bringing to 'justice' of witches as he was for his debauched cruelty, earning himself the name of The Black Judge.

Nice guy.

And The Black Mountain Inn? There couldn't be too many of them in the area, it had to be Geraint Meredith's place. Dark horse had kept that history to himself; obviously it was something he didn't want brought to light. But it had to be common knowledge. History like that never went untold, and was probably expanded down the years. Another pint at The Black Mountain Inn was due.

Hugo had stated that he had been involved in the black arts with his guest, who Mike now believed to be Judge Llewellyn. Bradney had stated that there was talk about The Black Judge being in league with the Devil. It fitted. No grey areas, the theory fitted with Hugo's journal at least.

So if the 'he' was in fact Sir Thomas Llewellyn then the child would surely be Eleanor's baby, Marie Katherine. And if it was the Judge who was coming for her, what did he want with her?

He didn't like the way his thoughts were leading. Surely to God this wasn't about the unspeakable? Whatever it was, Hugo was guilty of having been party to it, he had said as much in the journal. And later he had recanted and sent the child away to safety with the maid Zillah. And then he had killed the judge and buried him.

Mike returned to Bradney's text and continued reading. The following paragraphs were meagre pickings but then he read 'Sir Thomas Llewellyn disappeared on the thirtieth of April 1654. Local folklore tells that he died on Walpurgis Night, May Eve in 1645, when the Devil himself came for the Black Judge because he had failed him in some way.'

There could be no question; 'he' was Sir Thomas Llewellyn, the Black Judge. Mike's thoughts switched to Eleanor. If the Blue Lady was in fact Eleanor De Montefort then her anguished instructions to protect the child could have been her warning to Hugo which had created such an imprint in the atmosphere that the event was played and replayed, triggered by events happening in the present. Unless, as he suspected, the spirit of Eleanor was interactive, and therefore had intellect and could be categorised as a ghost rather than an imprint. He needed more.

Time to check out the crypt.

CHAPTER TWENTY: IN THE CRYPT

Mike flicked the switch at the head of the stone stairs. The steps were steep and narrow and curved away to the left which put pressure on his already painful leg. He took them slowly.

Just inside the door to the dimly lit crypt Mike's full spectrum video camera and tripod lay sideways on the floor. Next to them lay a broken digital recorder.

"Ah crap!"

He bent to pick up the pieces of the voice recorder and a small movement in the far corner caught his eye. He froze.

His eyes adjusted to the gloom and focussed on what looked like a bundle of white cloth in the corner. The bundle moved.

And so did Mike. He was on his feet in a heartbeat, despite the accompanying protest from his titanium filled leg. His heart was racing as he moved slowly forwards.

The white bundle was still moving and now the movement was accompanied by a stifled sob. Mike wasn't breathing as he took two more steps closer.

Through the gloom he could see the outline of a crouched figure, the source of the crying. He took another step closer.

The bundle let out a shriek that shrivelled the parts other shrieks didn't reach. And it flew through the semi darkness straight at Mike who was still not breathing and worried that his heart was coming through his ribcage.

Instinctively Mike grabbed the figure as it cannoned into him, logic processing the fact that the figure was solid. He held on.

"Hold on, let's get a look at you."

117

He turned into the light.

"Mary!"

She shrieked again and struggled for freedom, he released the strength of his hold on her not wanting to hurt her, but she was clearly bent on running so he held her arms by her side, anchoring her to the floor.

"Mary, it's me! Mike Travis. What are you doing down here? And what …" He looked at her closely. Her eyes were blank and staring, her face contorted into a mask of fear. She was still screaming but there was no sound.

"Jesus Mary," he said softly, "What happened to you? And where are your clothes?"

It registered for the first time the she was wearing nothing but a long white linen shift that clung to the folds of her ample body. He took a step back from her, still holding her wrists, firmly but gently.

"Mary, look at me. I'm going to let go of your arms so I can give you my jacket. You have to promise not to run. Do you understand?"

Mary's face remained contorted in the silent scream. Mike felt the resistance leave her as she sagged towards him. He lowered her to the floor and slipped off his jacket, putting it around her shoulders. She made no movement, no effort to clutch the jacket to her as would have been the normal reaction. She was deathly pale and he put his fingers to her throat. Her pulse was strong but erratic and fast. She appeared to be breathing in between the silent screams.

"Mary, I'm going to call for help. I'll be right back. Okay?"

Mary was unresponsive.

He made for the stair case; there was no way he would get a signal on his own phone down there. As his foot connected with the first step an icy blast hit him head on, taking his breath away. It lingered around him for a second and then seemed to go right through him into the crypt.

"Mary!"

He turned back as Mary stood up, her eyes sightless, her mind elsewhere, but still her silent screams seemed to echo around the walls. Mike swayed forwards but leaned against the stone wall and got a hold.

"Mary!" He grabbed her, there was no sign of recognition then as if a switch had been thrown, she lunged at him and the scream found its voice. Her face transformed from a scream into rage as spittle gathered at the corner of her mouth and she flew at Mike, scratching and snarling in the grip of some form of seizure.

"Jesus!"

He grabbed her again, and held her hard this time, but her strength had come from nowhere and she spat and raged at him taking all his strength to just hold her.

As quickly as it had begun, the seizure died down and once again she slumped to the floor. He checked her pulse again, there was no change and her breathing was slow but steady. She continued to stare sightlessly and appeared totally unaware of his presence.

He tried to run up the stairs but had to take them one at a time and slowly. In the hallway he grabbed his phone from his pocket. No signal. He hurried into the library and grabbed the telephone to dial 999.

"I need an ambulance please, St Winifride's Abbey. Please hurry, there's a young girl injured. I think … I think she's been attacked. You'd better send the police as well."

He put down the phone and headed back to the crypt. Mary hadn't moved but the spreading dark stain on the floor was evidence of her terror. Poor kid. What in God's name had happened to her?

The boyfriend. She'd obviously ignored his warning and gone to meet the bastard. Well, whoever it was better pray hard that the cops got to him first. Thank God she'd had the sense to come back to the Abbey before all rational thought had taken a vacation.

He could no longer kneel down or squat due to his ironmongery so he sat next to her ensuring a distance

119

between them, he didn't want to spook her again. Though who had spooked who remained in question.

"Mary, if you can hear me, I want you to know that help is coming. Do you think you can talk to me? Mary?"

She didn't respond.

Ten minutes later he heard the sirens in the distance and pushed himself upright and climbed the steps again. He opened the front door and left it wide and for the first time noticed how badly he was shaking. He rolled his head on his neck and took a deep breath, focussing on what was inevitable. His position looked dodgy. Injured girl frightened witless in the crypt, no-one else in the building except him, no-one to confirm that he hadn't touched her.

"Bollocks," he said to no-one in particular.

The blue lights were framed by the doorway and two paramedics were in the hallway at speed.

"She's down in the crypt, down those stairs. As far as I can tell she's not physically injured, but it's dark …" He was talking to air, the medics were already at the foot of the staircase, opening cases and leaning over Mary.

Another set of lights appeared beside the ambulance. He sighed, this could get nasty. Thank God Beth was oblivious in her bed.

The taller of the two medics reappeared and pushed past him through the door to the back of the ambulance to retrieve a stretcher but before he could return two policemen were in short conversation with him. He returned with the stretcher and disappeared back down into the crypt. Mike thought he might throw up.

The two cops, a sergeant and a constable, approached him calmly and deliberately as the medics wheeled the blanketed Mary, still staring vacantly, into the back of the ambulance that left the abbey with blues and twos.

The sergeant took his hat off and placed it under his arm. "Your name please, sir."

"Mike Travis. I know how this must look but …"

"What happened here?" the sergeant persisted.

"I'm here doing an investigation into the abbey and I went down into the crypt. It was only then that I became aware of Mary. She had some kind of seizure but now she seems catatonic. I don't know how she got into that state. I found her like it huddled in the cellar. I called you straight away."

The constable was taking notes while he listened. "Is there anyone else in the building, sir?"

Here we go. "No. In fact I believed myself to be alone. I had no idea that Mary was still here."

"Still?" This time from the sergeant.

Mike sighed; he knew what he would be thinking if their roles were reversed. "As far as I was aware, she left before noon. I can't be certain but it was around eleven. I've been here alone, or I thought I was, ever since then. I have no idea what happened to her."

The sergeant continued the grilling. "And your business here? You said you were conducting an investigation. Into what may I ask?"

"I'm a paranormal investigator. I have permission from the manager of the abbey to verify if possible whether or not the place is haunted."

Their faces said it all. The constable looked away briefly.

"Yep, that's right, ghost hunter, spook detective, whatever you want. But I have permission to be here. Mary is a member of staff, she's a domestic here. And I think you'd better come and sit down, this could take some time." He didn't wait for permission but returned to the library and sat at the desk. They followed in silence and sat at the other chairs around the desk facing him. This already felt like an interrogation.

"Do I need a solicitor?"

"That depends on what you have to tell us. Sir," replied the sergeant.

Mike told them everything.

The constable leaned across the desk. "The paramedics

have told us that there are no apparent physical injuries and no obvious signs of rape. The girl appears to have been terrified by something, or someone. She isn't talking. And there is no-one else to verify what you are saying."

Mike brightened suddenly. "But there is! My video cameras have been running constantly and there is one in the crypt. I found it knocked to the floor, but it's in a protective rubber jacket, it should still be running or if not, it may show Mary entering the crypt. And it automatically records the time which appears as a digital readout on the screen. The others should show my movements around the place."

He got to his feet, but the sergeant waved him back down. "We'll get that in a moment. In the meantime, is there anyone who can verify that you have permission to be here?"

"Gavin St. John Radford. He's the manager of the trust that owns the abbey. Here's his number."

Mike reached out for his phone and flicked a switch, there was still no signal.

"Maybe if you take it outside you'll get some action. His number is in my list of contacts. Be my guest. He handed his phone to the young constable who scraped his chair back and took the phone. He disappeared outside and in his absence Mike supplied the sergeant with his name, address, his contact number, practically everything bar his shoe size.

The constable returned and handed the phone back to Mike. "Mr. St. John Radford is not a happy man, I'm afraid. He does however confirm your story about why you are here and the fact that Mary does indeed work here as a cleaner. He also said that the girl has been acting strangely of late. I've spoken with the Inspector and in view of there being no apparent physical injuries to the girl, he's happy for you to return home but remain available. Mr. St. John Radford has asked that you leave the premises as arranged. Collect your equipment Mr.

Travis and pack up. We'll wait here until you've vacated the premises which may later become a crime scene. I have to ask you to report to Monmouth police station tomorrow to make a formal statement."

Mike breathed out in relief. He started to collect his bags ready to receive his equipment from around the abbey. It took less time to retrieve it all than it did to put it in place. He had left the camera in the crypt until last. The coppers had apparently forgotten about it. He packed it carefully in its protective case and zipped it up. One by one he took his bags to his car then returned to the library for his laptop. The cops were standing in the hallway watching him.

He zipped his laptop into its carrying case then without a glance around, he put the journal and The History of Monmouth and St. Winifride's Abbey: A History into the side pocket. He turned off the light.

The sergeant was outside, speaking into his radio. The young constable was watching him carefully. He put his head on one side.

"Seriously? Haunted?"

Mike thought for a moment then replied, "Yeah, I'd say the place is seriously haunted. Night."

He walked out and the young officer followed him and watched as Mike locked the doors. "I'm supposed to post the keys back through the letterbox," he said.

The cop's hand was outstretched, "I'll take them if you please, sir. As I said, this may become a crime scene." He held his hand out steady and Mike met his eyes. He dropped the keys into his hand.

"Thank you, sir. Tomorrow morning at the station if you please. Oh, and there appears to be four missed calls on your phone. Please don't return the calls while you're driving. Goodnight."

He stood watching Mike as he started his car and crawled it down the driveway. He stopped at the bottom and checked his phone.

An unfamiliar number and three from Beth.

He selected her messages and listened to her voice, fragile and scared and disorientated. He listened to the second message. What the hell was happening?

He made a decision and before flooring the accelerator he made a call. It wasn't to Beth.

CHAPTER TWENTY ONE: VIDEO RECORDING

The cottage was in darkness as Mike pulled into the garage. It was a good sign. Beth was obviously in bed and asleep. He checked his watch. It was one a.m., hours before he was due to be home.

He let himself in quietly and flicked on the light; there was no sound from upstairs. He went straight through to the dining room and over to the old oak sideboard they'd found in an antique shop in Abergavenny and poured a hefty glass of whisky and then sat down on the sofa, sipping and thinking.

He stood in a precarious position and if the police decided that Mary had been assaulted in any way… He couldn't get the picture of her blank staring eyes out of his head.

He stood suddenly and made for the stairs, slipping out of his shoes as he headed for their bedroom. The door stood slightly ajar and he pushed it tentatively, willing it to be silent. It obeyed.

Beth was lying under the quilt, dishevelled and breathing heavily, she was restless but seemed to be in a deep sleep. She moaned and he stood still, unwilling to wake her. She turned onto her side and murmured in her sleep. He caught the words 'Adain' and 'brook'. She gave a small cry and tossed her head from side to side. He was reluctant to wake her but went to her side in case she should wake from the dream that troubled her. After a few minutes she seemed to settle again and he bent low over her and kissed her on her cheek. She mumbled a few incoherent words and then sank back into the arms of quiet sleep.

Mike tiptoed back out of the room and slipped his shoes back on at the foot of the stairs. The video recorder from the crypt was still in the car. He needed to see what, if anything, had recorded.

He set up his laptop in his study and closed the door carefully. He didn't want Beth to wake to the sounds of Mary's screams before they had become silent ones. Then deciding to play it safe he attached the headphones. Beth needed her sleep and he needed time to examine what had happened back there.

Her message was still uppermost in his mind. She was obviously very disturbed about the woman that she kept seeing and it was obvious from her message that she believed the woman to be a ghost.

He hadn't seen the woman, but that meant nothing. There were some ghosts he saw and some he didn't. If she was indeed in spirit, then it appeared as if she was attached to Beth in some way, maybe even trying to communicate with her.

Whatever, Beth was upset and she was vulnerable right then. Her perceptions were either deadly accurate or they were skewed by hormones. Whichever, he was going to minimise the upset to her and had done his best to achieve that with the phone call he had made on the way out of the abbey.

He pressed 'play' on the video recorder.

The picture split into two screens. One was a straight recording capturing images from the semi darkness of the crypt. Mike believed in conducting his investigations in the normal light for the area and so he had left the safety lights on and no others. The second screen appeared in a kaleidoscope of coloured shapes. It was a thermal image of anything in the crypt that moved or was static.

He froze the thermal image wanting to examine each one closely. The other recording began to play out. Nothing happened, nothing moved and there were no light anomalies. The recorded time in the bottom left of the

126

screen scrolled on. He had no idea what time Mary had appeared in the crypt, only that it was around eleven thirty when he'd gone to check it out. He watched nothing happening for almost an hour and a half and he could feel his eyelids getting heavy.

Mike was suddenly alert as a shadow movement appeared at the top of the stairs. He noted the time recorded in the bottom right hand corner of the screen; it was ten forty.

Mary's bare foot appeared on the stone steps and he watched her appear fully. She was looking sideways and was beaming happily. He slowed the recording. She appeared to be looking directly at someone. Someone who wasn't there.

So, the boyfriend was of an imaginary nature?

Mary continued to descend into the crypt, still beaming happily. Unfortunately her thin white shift clung to her and Mike was embarrassed and felt like a voyeur, but he had to see what was unfolding.

At the foot of the stairs she turned sideways and Mike quickly stopped the recording and rewound it slightly. Mary turned sideways again and this time Mike hit the pause button. He leaned in close to the screen, peered hard at it for a minute or so and then hit a few more buttons on the control panel, tweaking and enhancing the optimum light on the image. He felt himself pale as his eyes confirmed his impression.

Next to Mary was a large black formless shadow which appeared to be wrapped around her.

He let the recording continue and watched in shock as the shadow appeared to lift Mary into the air and carry her to a stone tomb and drop her on top of it.

"No!" he yelled, then quickly put his hand over his mouth less he blurt out more and possibly wake Beth. Not an imaginary boyfriend, this was something terrible, an incubus at the very least. A demon, sometimes in physical male form, sometimes in spirit, who ravished and raped women.

His skin was crawling and he felt sick but he had to continue to watch what had happened to Mary. For her. He was glad he'd taken the whisky bottle into the study with him. It was going to take a hit.

At first glance Mary appeared to float on her back through the air and then hit the tombstone hard. He slowed the recording and saw the impact. It had to have hurt. He swallowed a mouthful of whisky that hit the back of his throat like a laser.

The shadow grew darker as Mike watched and it would now be visible even to an untrained onlooker. He was relieved. Even the police would have to take notice of it. Not understand it, and have the recording examined for hours on end to ensure it hadn't been tampered with. That he hadn't tampered with it.

But they would find themselves having to take it on face value. He guessed it would be hastily buried.

He felt a tight grip around his chest as Mary's shift appeared to hike itself up above her waist.

"Oh Jesus! No. Please God, no!"

He couldn't do it. He couldn't watch the violation. He'd leave that for the cops.

Instead he fast forwarded the recording to its end and then rewound it on screen.

He watched himself walk backwards down the steps and sit back down beside Mary. The scratching and spitting followed. He continued to rewind until the screen showed the traumatised Mary huddled in the corner. He slowed it down but let it rewind. After a few minutes Mary screamed and her hands flew up in front of her face in a protective shield. Mike ground his teeth.

He expected to see her walk or crawl to the corner, but he shut his eyes as her crumpled body sailed through the air and hit the far wall then slide into the heap in the corner.

Mike slammed his glass hard onto his desk, splashing

the whisky over the back of his violently shaking hand. He hit the control panel again and the thermal image screen appeared.

Mary's figure appeared on the stairs, a blend of red, oranges and yellows. Her feet appeared as blue blotches. The poor kid's feet were cold. It made Mike even angrier if that were possible.

As she descended the staircase there was another figure beside her. This figure was almost an artwork of differing hues of blue. Indicating only varying degrees of ice cold. Mike swallowed.

Whoever was with Mary was not of this world.

He made a sudden decision. Morning was too far away. He needed to take this to the cops right then.

He paused momentarily; he'd had several belts of scotch and was way over the limit. But he knew another whole bottle would be unable to make him anywhere approaching drunk. He grabbed his laptop and recorder and left.

CHAPTER TWENTY TWO: DROWNED

Brookstone 1654

Adain, was being pulled roughly from the horse and marched towards her cottage. She had a large swelling and a bruise on her cheek; someone had cut up rough. She staggered as the man yanked on her arms, still tied, and almost threw her inside.

Seated by the side of the fire was a large man with a long brown curled wig. He had a ruddy complexion and a long aquiline nose which enhanced his weasel like features. He was dressed in the manner of a man of the privileged class which his huge belly testified to and Adain knew at once that this was the infamous judge, Sir Thomas Llewellyn.

She was thrown roughly onto the flagstone floor.

The judge looked down his sharp nosed features at her, considering her, boring into her, his large flabby tongue licking the thin dry lips.

Adain chose not to allow him to see her fear.

"Something aileth you, my lord? Your man informeth me that you require a healing draught?"

He considered her some more and then said, "You owneth such powers, wench?"

Caught between two dire outcomes, she chose the truth. "I hath knowledge of the healing properties in God's plants and flowers, it is so."

He stared at her longer and she cringed as he ran his bloated tongue across his thin lips again.

He leaned forwards, his face too close to hers, "It is said that such knowledge cometh only from consorting with the Devil. How sayeth you?"

131

"Surely, sire, it is God that hath set the plants on this earth and only he owneth such knowledge to impart."

"Believeth you to be chosen by God to be understanding of his works? Blasphemy at best, witchcraft at worst. Stand!"

Adain struggled to her feet and stood before him, chin forward in defiance. If she were to die, she would not cower before the lecher.

He stood also; close enough for her to detect the odour of disease. She continued her defiance.

"Sire, it is the truth that I have helped another with what aileth you. The herbs I have, here in my kitchen and in my garden. Wilt thou allow me to alleviate your suffering?"

He looked over at the man that had brought her, "Free her from the bonds, man," he rasped as he nodded his dismissal.

"Perchance you own such knowledge, but also I see that hast other skills at thou disposal." He looked down at the first signs of her pregnancy in her belly and laid his fat hand on her breast pressing it against the outline of her body and coming to rest over her swollen belly.

She felt her resolve slowly dissipating as she wanted to vomit.

Her mind was reeling as she sought escape from what was clearly now uppermost in the judges mind as he began removing his coat. A glance outside showed her the horsemen had removed themselves from her garden and were waiting on the dirt road that lead back into Monmouth. The decision made, she bolted through the door and down to the brook.

The judge was a heavy set man despite his mean features but poxed or not, he caught her as she made for the little bridge. His was breathless and his chest was heaving dangerously but he overpowered her with his sheer bulk and in short moments had ripped off her bodice and skirt.

She was beneath him, struggling for breath and freedom, her mind racing through all possibilities amidst prayers for salvation, when he tumbled her into the deepest part of the brook.

She freed an arm and had clawed his face before she realised what she had done. Her floundering hand connected with a chain around his neck and she pulled it hard, hoping to exert enough pressure around his own throat to give her a moment's respite. The ornate locket bearing his crest came away in her hand.

Enraged beyond lust, Thomas Llewellyn had his hands around her throat and was squeezing hard and keeping her under the surface of the brook. He was unaware of the horseman running through the garden as the last of her breath bubbled up through the water.

"Sire?"

The bloated judge released her and watched as the water lapped over her open sightless eyes.

"Rid me of it," he spluttered. "Then seek out the man and escort him to my chamber at the inn. My horse!" he demanded as he stamped off up the garden to the gate.

The horseman looked around him until he saw Adain's spade, he grabbed it and then pulled Adain from the water, threw her across his shoulder and crossed the bridge.

He walked for as long as he could bear her dead weight and the water dripping down his back, then in a small clearing to the left of the path he dug her grave.

Later, in another clearing deeper in the forest Owain was surprised by four men on horseback and unable to resist was swiftly knocked to the ground and bound by the hands and gagged. He was tied to the saddle of the leading horse and dragged through the forest and out onto the dirt road that took them to the Black Mountain Inn.

Hours later plumes of smoke and flames were seen coming from the middle of the woods. The charcoal pit had consumed the timbers and they were burning out.

At that moment Owain stood, shackled and bleeding,

confused and disorientated in the court room of the inn. Sir Thomas Llewellyn was placing the black cap on his head.

"Owain ap Rhys, thou hast been proven guilty of the heinous crime of murder. Thou hast brutally slaughtered thy wife. And thou hast been also proven as consorting with a witch, thy wife. Thou shallt be taken from this place and be hanged until thou art dead. There shall be no mercy on thy soul."

The information filtered slowly through Owain's addled mind. Adain? His beautiful Adain was dead? And their child?

His tortured cry filled the inn and he was grasped from behind and thrown into a holding room adjacent to the court room. There had been no trial, he had been declared guilty even as Adain's poor body was being buried in the woods.

Fifteen minutes later the rope was creaking against the beam above the stairwell and Owain was reunited with his Adain.

CHAPTER TWENTY THREE:
WELCOME GUEST

Beth opened her eyes feeling groggy. Her dream was still vivid and even in her waking confusion she knew it was more than that. Her head ached and she felt slightly sick. A glance at the clock told her it was four thirty in the morning and the insistent signal from her bladder told her it was time to visit the loo pronto.

She stumbled back to bed and turned on her side, the most comfortable way since she'd been six months pregnant.

And in minutes she was back in the dream.

She watched from the boundaries of her dream as Adain struggled with the man. She watched from the safety of sleep as she was drowned and then buried. She watched from the innocence of the onlooker as Owain was tried, found guilty and sentenced to his death in the span of a heartbeat. She watched from the confines of nightmare as his body swung at the end of the rope, casting long shadows around the hall of an old inn.

She sat bolt upright, there was a noise downstairs. Her heart thumped in her breast and she held her breath, still in the delirium of the dream.

The clinging hands of sleep left her slowly and she recognised the sound. A key in the door and the door closing. Mike was home.

The sigh of relief escaped her and she threw back the quilt and swung her legs over the edge of the bed and wriggled her toes into her slippers.

"Mike?" she called out.

"Yeah, baby," he replied from half way up the stairs.

He was in the doorway before she had pulled on her

135

dressing gown.

"Oh my God! You look like hell! Are you okay?" She was across the room, her arms around him before he could answer, her dream receding at speed as she probed her husband's eyes for reassurance.

"Mike?"

He hugged her, relishing her warmth and the hint of her perfume, the silkiness of her hair, the feel of goodness after his contact with something unclean. The thought made him pull away, unwilling to contaminate her. He planted a kiss on her forehead.

"I need a long shower. I'll tell you about it over coffee." *But not all of it.* He looked hard at her. "You look tired. Get back into bed and I'll bring coffee and toast when I've cleaned up."

She shook her head. "No chance. Get your shower and I'll see you downstairs, and before you start, I mean it. You know I make better coffee than you do. You've got fifteen minutes, then I'm coming to get you."

He grinned at her, normality seeping into his pores, turning the events of the night into what seemed like distant memory. If only.

Beth waddled through the living room and dining room and into the kitchen to fill the kettle. Her mind was running rampant with images of Adain in life and death and of the long shadows cast by Owain's swinging body. A nightmare surely? She was over tired and anxious since the midwife's visit. She had much to tell Mike, but from his demeanour it was obvious that he had anxieties of his own. But with the prospect of giving birth within a week, she didn't have the luxury of waiting until he'd got his worries off his chest. She'd tell him over breakfast.

As she turned to reach for the bread crock, the slapping wet sound she'd heard previously came from behind her. She froze. Surely now she knew the source of the sound. Very slowly she turned around.

Adain stood behind her, softly weeping and dripping

onto the kitchen floor.

Beth dropped the bread crock with a loud crash and staggered backwards against the worktop.

The shade of Adain began to fade, but not before Beth heard her say, "I'm sorry. I seeketh not to afear thee. But to warn thee. And to beseech thee to seek my grave for I rest not. I am sorry. "

Beth stood among the remains of the bread crock unable to move or to speak as Mike thundered painfully down the stairs, the second dripping wet figure to appear before her. He took her by the arm and pulled her to him.

"Beth? What is it? Tell me! Are you in pain? What?"

She couldn't answer him, leaning against him, ashen and shaking.

He guided her through into the living room and sat her down on the sofa oblivious to the fact he was naked and soaking wet from the shower, shampoo still lathered in his hair.

"Beth? Talk to me."

"I'm sorry, Mike. I didn't mean to scare you. It's just … just …" She poured it all out to him as he sat next to her, arm around her shoulders as she told him about her dreams, about the bridge, the TV, the pain in her temple whenever Adain appeared by the bridge, about the footprints and about Adain standing before her in the kitchen. She told him about the midwife calling on her and her high blood pressure and the fact that their baby was to put in an appearance sooner than they had thought.

He sat in silence while she poured it all out to him, the weight of the universe slowly descending on his shoulders as he gently squeezed her shoulder. Eventually he said, "Right. Put your feet up. I'm going to get dressed and make breakfast. Then I'm going to ring Jack and cancel his visit."

She'd forgotten that Jack was due there that evening. "No, please don't. I could do with some normality around here. What about you? What happened at the abbey?

You're home earlier than I expected." He didn't reply. "Mike? What happened, please tell me? I'll worry more if you don't tell me."

"Nothing for you to worry about," he said softly.

"Now I'm worried. You'd better tell me."

"Okay. But breakfast first. You've got to feed that daughter of ours," he said lightly, trying to sound casual. It was the first time that he'd acknowledged that their child was a girl.

They ate in silence, each watching the other for signs of anxiety. Mike was the first to speak.

"Well, I think I can safely say that the abbey is definitely home to unquiet spirits." He gave her an abridged version, leaving out the more harrowing details of Mary's attack.

She was pale and put a hand to his face. "Oh my God. What happened at the police station?"

"Well, at first it was just me and the sergeant that came out to the abbey, then an Inspector James came in and watched the recording. Before it had finished there must have been half a dozen in there with us. At first the Inspector was fairly derogatory about the paranormal; I didn't expect much else to be honest. But that soon changed as they watched it. They kept my laptop and the recorder to get their computer experts to check that I haven't removed anything or doctored the recording. I expected that too. Look Beth, I don't want you having this on your mind right now. It's going to be all right."

"But?"

"But I think there's more. I haven't got the whole picture yet and I think I'm going to leave it that way, at least until after the baby comes. You're my priority right now." He was suddenly thankful for the phone call he had made on his way home. He decided not to tell her about it yet.

"Please don't stop Jack from coming. It'll be good for you after last night, and I want to meet him. We're going to need a godfather for this one you know." She seemed thoughtful, "Mike why don't you call your father. Surely it's time to put old bones to bed?"

He stood up suddenly. "Leave it, Beth. I told you, I don't want anything to do with him, okay?"

"You've never told me what came between you, love. Was it so terrible?"

Mike was white, "If you must know he had an affair. It destroyed my mother and soon afterwards she was diagnosed with cancer and she died. That's all there is to it. He killed her, Beth. As surely as if he'd put a gun to her head. Now, leave it. Please?"

She nodded sadly at him, seeing the old hurt begin it's gnawing at him all over again and was instantly sorry for opening up the old wound. "I'm sorry," she said quietly.

He nodded at her. "I'm going upstairs to make up a room for Jack, if you're sure that is."

She smiled at him. "Of course I'm sure. He sounds like a breath of fresh air. And Mike, I'm fine. Stop worrying. It's not as if I hadn't dealt with this sort of thing before. Crowsmoor was baptism by fire. It'll be okay."

He bent and kissed her on the top of her head. "Okay, baby. Now put your feet up and rest. Call me if you need anything."

She heard him moving about upstairs and lay back against the cushion. A cloud flitted across her face as she pondered Mike's broken relationship with his father. He was obviously bitter and there was no forgiveness in his heart and she was sorry for it. Forgiveness had a habit of healing.

They passed the afternoon cuddled together on the sofa watching old movies, though neither of them was really focussed on the plots that they knew by heart. Around four, she said, "What about dinner, love? I don't want Jack coming to egg and chips."

He laughed, "Actually, egg and chips is Jack's favourite but don't panic, I told you, I'll order a take out."

139

"There's no wine here and the whisky looks low," she said.

Mike looked at his watch. "Good thinking, I'll go to the shop and sort that out. If you're okay, that is."

"Don't fuss so; I'm fine now I've told you all about it. And now I know why Adain isn't at peace. I know, Mike. I know where she's buried. We have to do something about that."

"Yeah, but not now. When all this is over and the baby's here and settled, then I'll go and talk to Inspector James again. I saw his face, didn't say much but he's opening up to the idea of restless spirits now. He'll do things properly. I won't be long. I'm going into Monmouth to order food from the Italian place on the High Street, and I'll pay them extra to deliver it and there's a decent off licence right next door. Stay put."

Beth settled back against the sofa again, relieved to have told Mike everything, it seemed less traumatic as she put it all into words. She thought about Adain's presence in the kitchen and her words. She'd said she wanted to warn her. Warn her about what? She shook her head to clear the questions mounting in her head. Enough for that day. She flicked on the TV again then said out loud, "I don't know if you can hear me, Adain. But I want you to know we're going to sort it out. I know what happened to you, and I saw where he buried you. Give me some time, please, and then we'll bring it all to light and hopefully you can rest."

The TV turned over to a different channel. It was a programme about baptism. Something she had done many times while she was a vicar. And something now that was dear to her heart.

"Adain?"

The volume increased on the TV of its own volition, as if to say, 'listen'.

Her mind wandered to Mike's account of Hugo De Montefort's journal and how he had taken his daughter to the chapel and baptised her himself in the name of God. She wondered what he was afraid of. Mike hadn't told her everything, she was sure of it. She knew that De Montefort had been involved with the dark arts but had recanted. Was he afraid for his daughter? Did he think that the man he was afraid of would come and take her? Why? What hadn't Mike told her?

The TV got louder.

She sat up suddenly. She knew. She didn't know why she knew, but she knew what he was afraid of. The man he feared was going to take his daughter and baptise her to the Devil. The words in her head ran back to back.

A life for a life.

She couldn't bear to think of such things, though she knew from experience that such men had no scruples when it came to appeasing their dark master. She must talk to Mike. But not tonight. There was, after all, nothing he could do centuries on. Whatever had been done back then had been done, and there was no undoing history.

The TV turned itself off.

She sighed and settled back and closed her eyes, suddenly weary. She would meet Jack and eat with them, and then take herself to bed early, safe in the knowledge that Mike was only yards away. The thought comforted her and she allowed herself to drift off into a peaceful doze with no dreams.

She woke to voices. Mike was back, but obviously not alone. She strained to hear the voice as she stood up and tried to tidy her hair, frustrated at not having had the time to change. She'd not expected Jack quite this early.

Mike came into the room, beaming. "I've got a surprise for you."

Beth fixed her eyes on the door, and then gave a cry of delight as a solid looking woman with steel grey hair, wearing a tweed skirt and sensible shoes came into the room.

"Martha!" Beth squealed with delight and threw herself

141

at her visitor.

"Wanted to visit. Michael said now was a good time."

CHAPTER TWENTY FOUR: JACK

Martha Treneglos extricated herself deftly from Beth's extended hug. Mike smiled as he detected the hint of a flush on the older woman's cheek; the best to be hoped for as an expression of any emotion.

Mike's voice was warm with genuine affection, "Welcome to our little cottage, Martha. Sit down and make yourself at home."

"Oh, I am so pleased to see you!" Beth continued, "Mike! Why didn't you tell me? I would have made the other room up. I would have …"

"And that's exactly why I didn't tell you. I made the other room up this morning when I did Jack's. I'm afraid he'll have to make do with the box room. He's only staying the night."

Beth looked perplexed, "But when …?"

"Martha and I made arrangements for her visit weeks ago as a surprise, but things kinda made me bring it forward. I called her last night and she was on the train this morning."

Martha snorted. "If you can call it that! Damn thing went too fast. No corridors. No compartments. Tea like camel's water and vile sandwiches!"

Mike hid a smile; he wondered when the last time was that Martha had travelled anywhere, let alone by train. It must have come as a shock.

A sudden thought crossed his mind. "Er Martha, what about Cat? Who's looking after him?" He dreaded the answer, picturing her boxes that were still in the back of his car.

"Hmph. Damn fool cat. Took on a tourist's Rottweiler. Spent the last of his nine. Put up a fight though."

Mike pictured the sullen tabby that had an inborn dislike of all human and canine life. All except Martha that was. He didn't doubt for a moment that the Rottweiler had left the scene worse for wear.

"Oh, poor Cat," said Beth. "I'm so sorry, Martha."

"Yes, well. Daft bugger was old, should've known better. Took the damn dog's ear off though," she said with an almost satisfied smile as she settled into an armchair.

"Well, I can't promise you Lipton's best," said Mike suddenly as he tried to break the mood. "But it won't be camel's water. I'll see to it." He put up a hand to Beth before she could get up, and disappeared into the kitchen.

"Oh, Martha, I can't tell you how glad I am to see you." She meant it. If anyone could bring a steady no nonsense light on their lives right then it was Martha. Seventy two years old with a mind like a bacon slicer, Martha had been the headmistress of a Cornish village school until she'd retired. It was all she'd known, teaching in that school. Then Deputy Head and eventually the fiercest, cleverest and most compassionate Head the school had ever known or would know again, though she had kept the compassion well hidden from her students who had nothing but respect for her. Beth knew why.

Martha was eyeing Beth closely, her eyes were like gimlets, piercing and probing. "So, you've got yourself into some more bother. Nothing he can't handle," she said nodding towards the kitchen. "High blood pressure? Nonsense. Just need a damn good rest, girl."

"The midwife left me some tablets, I've been having headaches but I thought that was due to … something else."

"Hm. Michael told me about the something else."

"I'll tell you all about it in the morning, I just want to enjoy being with you tonight. Is that okay?"

"Of course."

Beth heard a car pull up into their driveway and was about to call Mike when he appeared with a tea tray just as the doorbell chimed.

"Aha! Jack! Don't worry, Martha, you'll love him!"

Martha perceived that as an extravagant assessment but was perhaps prepared to give the guy a chance at approval at least.

Beth smiled at the obvious pleasure on Mike's face as he went to greet his friend. When he returned he had his hand on Jack's shoulder and was beaming widely. She hadn't realised until then how much they had meant to one another.

Jack was every bit like the photograph she'd seen of him. Tall and well built with sandy hair that had been obviously cut by an exclusive hairdresser, although he was decidedly more tanned than in his picture. His deep tan accentuated his good looks and the gold locket that he always wore around his neck. It had been a gift from his mother just before he was deployed to Afghanistan and contained a consecrate communion wafer. Her way of keeping him safe whilst he was in a war zone.

Beth thought he wouldn't be out of place on a beach, toting a surf board. His green eyes flashed in obvious pleasure and it translated to a wicked grin. He had a huge bouquet of flowers and wine in his hand. Mike carried another two bottles, the rest of Jack's offering.

In two strides, Jack had crossed the room and had Beth in a bear hug, squashing the flowers.

He released her and then gave her a peck on the cheek. "Pleased to meet you, Mrs. Travis. Never thought I'd see the day when I'd be saying that to anyone!" He turned to Mike, "You sly old dog. You said she was beautiful, but that was an understatement! And another beautiful lady as well."

Mike laughed. "Jack Carter, allow me to introduce our friend, Martha Treneglos. Martha, this reprobate is my friend Jack. Don't believe a single word that he tells you about me. Nor you!" he said, laughing towards Beth.

Jack released the flowers into Beth's arms and took

Martha's hand. He bent low over it and kissed it.

"A pleasure to meet you ma'am. How very fortunate I am to be in such lovely company tonight."

Mike waited for the retort that would surely come from Martha, but had to suppress a smile when instead, she became quite flustered. And the hint of a flush that had appeared before, now took centre stage. He clapped Jack on the back.

"Steady on, Jack. She'll soon see through you and then you've had it."

Martha stood up hastily. "Michael, perhaps you'd give me a hand with my case and boxes, there's a good lad."

Mike eyed the boxes suspiciously. Images of Crowsmoor with Martha brandishing her father's World War 2 pistol came into his mind. No, she wouldn't have. Martha saw his expression.

"Books," she said quickly. Just books."

Jack jumped to his feet. "You stay there, Martha, may I call you Martha? I'll help Mike with your luggage and leave you two lovely ladies to chat. But I warn you, I won't be gone long."

Martha snorted again at his retreating back. "Reminds me of Alex Trefusis. All charm and smiles. Caught him many a time with a cigarette. Never could give the damn boy detention."

Beth laughed. She could picture the scene.

Mike and Jack reappeared in short order and went straight through to the dining room. Beth heard the chink of her best china and glasses and relaxed. They finished setting the table just in time as the doorbell chimed again announcing dinner was delivered.

Jack went to answer the door and they could hear him conversing in fluent Italian with the delivery guy. Of course he did. Beth liked him already, and categorised him as loveable rogue. But she knew there was more to Jack than that from Mike. He had a very serious side and a sensitive nature that he hid behind the disguise of Jack the

Lad. She knew that during his time with Mike in Afghanistan he had flown more missions than anyone else into hostile territory. And she knew that when Mike had crashed, Jack had been beside him for days while Mike was kept under sedation, and he had been there for him through all the surgery and rehabilitation. Jack was a friend in the truest meaning of the word.

And she wanted him to be godfather to their baby. She knew that it would please Mike above all, but she had taken an instant liking to Jack too.

They enjoyed dinner immensely and Jack was at his animated best. Inevitably the conversation turned to the paranormal.

"So, Spooky, how many ghosts have you laid? And I mean that in the best possible way," he laughed.

Mike shifted in his chair. "You don't want to hear about that."

"Oh. But I do. Tell me about it, I'm really interested. I'll admit when you first got into all that stuff, I thought you'd lost the plot, but I want to know. I've seen some of the programmes on the telly; I never missed an episode of yours. So, are the programmes for real?"

Mike smiled. "Well, I believe a couple of them have the best intentions but some of their methods are a little less than scientific. Using the equipment doesn't make it a scientific investigation unless there is proven evidence. Personal experience doesn't count unless there's video or audio evidence. And there should be adequate controls in place."

"So do you go creeping around old houses in the dark?"

"Nope. I know most of the TV shows do that but it's really only good for dramatic effect, it doesn't make good sense. It's like chaining a rock to a runner, it's counter productive. Think about it; is it better to look for something in light or darkness? And most 'ghosts' are seen as misty apparitions or shadow figures. Is it easier to see a moving shadow in the dark, even with the night vision stuff, or in the light? And ghosts are seen both by day and night, so there is nothing to suggest that ghosts only come out at night or in the dark."

"So what are you into right now?"

Mike and Beth were quiet.

"Oh oh. Put my foot in it?"

Beth smiled and put her hand over his. "It's okay. I'm a bit touchy about a few things right now and Mike's investigation last night ended with him visiting the police station."

Jack whistled. "So what happened?"

Mike recounted the events of the previous evening, editing it here and there for Beth's benefit, not wanting to worry or upset her unduly. Her nerves were shattered as it was.

Further conversation was interrupted by the doorbell chiming. Mike went to answer it, noting Beth's anxious expression as he passed her.

They heard voices in the hallway and Mike reappeared with a tall, balding man in a crumpled grey suit and a world weary expression.

"This is Inspector James," Mike said by way of introduction. He's returning my laptop and recorder. And he just needs a chat with me, so if you'll excuse me for a moment."

Inspector James nodded amenably at them.

They disappeared into Mike's study and he closed the door. Beth was fidgety.

"Getting late. Time you were resting, my girl," said Martha. "We'll see to this," she said nodding in Jack's direction.

He stood up quickly, a little too quickly to allow for the amount of alcohol he had enjoyed, "Absolutely."

"Bed." Martha's order brooked no argument even if Beth had the energy to do so.

She smiled gratefully. "Thank you. Will you excuse me

Jack? It's been so lovely meeting you, you must come often. Mike and I will be happy to see you."

Jack beamed in genuine pleasure and leaned over and kissed her cheek. "Mind how you go, Beth. I probably won't see you in the morning, I'll be creeping out early, I've an important client to butter up tomorrow. Thank you for having me, especially now."

Martha followed her up the narrow stairs and put her hand on Beth's arm outside her door.

"Worried about you. You look more than tired. Calling the doctor in the morning if you're no better." She squeezed Beth's arm and headed back downstairs to clear up.

Jack had already made a start and was elbow deep in suds in the kitchen sink.

Martha eyed him carefully. "How good a friend are you, Jack Carter?"

Jack looked surprised. "Er, as good as I can be."

Martha nodded. "Good. I think he's going to need you."

CHAPTER TWENTY FIVE: A PHONE MESSAGE

Mike turned onto his side and propped himself up on his elbow. Daylight had begun to fill their room and he remained still, watching Beth sleep. He suddenly felt an overwhelming dread.

"I don't care if I have to go to Hell and back, I'll never let any harm come to you. Either of you."

"Mm," she murmured as she tried unsuccessfully to turn over to him, bringing a grin to his face. He stroked her forehead pleased that there were no outward signs of haunting dreams.

She opened her eyes as there was a discreet knock on their door.

Martha entered their room on Mike's invitation. She carried a tray laden with bacon, eggs and toast, orange juice and a pot of tea.

"Have to have a good breakfast."

"That's very sweet of you, Martha. But you're our guest." Mike said with a grin.

"Nonsense. My pleasure."

"We usually make do with muesli and coffee, lately."

Martha snorted her disapproval. "Horse feed."

Beth sat up, completely awake then. "Oh. Martha, this is lovely. I was hoping to get breakfast for you, this morning. You're here to visit, not look after me."

"Need your rest, girl. Going to see to it."

Beth smiled at her with affection. "Thank you."

Martha left them quickly and they turned their attention to the tray. Despite it being early they both realised that they could in fact do justice to the breakfast feast in front of them.

Mike poured their second cup of tea. "I need to talk to you about something, baby."

"Oh oh. Need I be worried?" she teased.

"Serious," he said, putting on the appropriate face.

"Okay," she kissed him on the cheek and shifted uncomfortably, pulling a face.

Mike sat up quickly. "What?"

She smiled at him. "A twinge. It's nothing."

"Need *I* be worried?"

"Absolutely. But I'll tell you when to panic. Now, what were you saying?"

He frowned. "I have to go out this morning. I wouldn't go, but I think you're in good hands. I won't be any longer than I need to be. Inspector James wants to go through the Abbey this morning, trying to reconstruct what happened there last night. It wasn't a casual invitation. I don't have a choice."

"Then you have to go. I'll be fine. I'm looking forward to catching up with Martha, this morning." She paused thoughtfully, "Mike, this *will* be all right, won't it?"

He nodded. "Of course. This is about policemen trying to make sense of what they don't understand, what none of us understands, not really."

"Be careful?"

"Always. Now, wench, I'm for the shower, *you* are for laying back down and resting."

Inspector James had timed the summons for eleven, an hour's drive minimum which gave him time to call on the landlord of the Black Mountain Inn. He had two reasons. The information the night before had led him to believe that Hugo De Montefort had killed and buried Sir Thomas Llewellyn there. And then there was the other message on his phone the night before. The one he hadn't told Beth about.

Beth and Martha had gone to bed and he and Jack had settled down to some serious drinking and some serious talking. Jack was fascinated to hear of the events at the

Abbey and what had happened in Crowsmoor. Alcohol enhanced his enthusiasm for the subject and he listened avidly.

Eventually, Jack had succumbed to tiredness and alcohol and had somehow made it up the stairs to his bedroom. Mike had listened to the last message on his phone.

"Mr Travis, this is Brian Jenkins. I keep the antique book store on the High Street in town. I'm calling you because I know of your interest in the subject of demonology and the dark arts. A man came into my shop today. He brought a book for sale. One that I daren't even put on my shelves. I need to speak with you urgently, before the book gets into the wrong hands. The book was brought to me by Geraint Meredith, the landlord of the Black Mountain Inn. I think you understand how important it is to keep this filthy book out of circulation. Please call me, regardless of the time. I'll be waiting to talk to you."

Mike had called him around one in the morning and was unsurprised by the immediate answer. Brian Jenkins had been waiting for his call.

"Mr. Jenkins? Mike Travis. I'm so sorry to call you so late. I'm intrigued by your call."

"I have no time for lengthy explanations, Mr. Travis; please listen very carefully to me. The landlord of the Black Mountain Inn has unearthed a tortuous evil. He is in possession of a book which has the power to bring a legion from the hell onto the earth..."

"Sorry, who did you say you were?" Mike interrupted.

"Please, Mr. Travis. Listen to me, there is little time. He plans to sell the book to someone who will use it to its most evil potential. You have to go there before he can take the book to Solomon Kingston in the High Street who will most certainly have such a buyer."

"Forgive me, but how do you know all this?"

"Because only yesterday he brought the book to me."

"If the book is such a big deal, why did you let it go? Why not buy it and be done?"

"Because I am not permitted to touch such a book."

"Not permitted?"

"It's up to you now, Mr. Travis. Goodbye."

"Wait …at least tell me which book."

"The Grimoire of Astaroth."

The persistent tone from the telephone announced the cut off. He redialled the number. It rang unanswered.

The conversation was still heavy on Mike's mind as he showered; trawling his memory for filed away information. He had studied demonology whilst lying broken in a hospital bed. It had followed on naturally from his other quest. To understand his death and return and to find out what happened in between. There was no logic in understanding one side and not the other but understanding didn't mean following.

Astaroth was a demon of the first hierarchy, a very powerful demon, a seducer. He was said to lead men to treasure and would answer any question put to him. A handy kind of guy to have around, if he hadn't been a demon of the pit.

So The Grimoire of Astaroth was probably some heavy text on the dark arts and ritual magic. And once again he was getting involved in something beyond human evil. He rubbed the shampoo into his scalp harder. He should walk away from it. He had Beth and their baby to consider. The guy on the phone was probably some religious extremist starting a panic about nothing. The medieval grimoires were rarely anything more than props for the gentry of that time to play dress up and satisfy their own perversions. The shampoo found its way into his eyes.

"Damn!" He squeezed his eyes shut and reached blindly for a towel.

"Here," Beth laughed as she put the towel in his hand. "I've got some of that no tears stuff ready for the baby, you should give it a go."

He muttered something from within the folds of the towel as he tried to clear his stinging eyes. Beth watched him quietly, taking in the horrendous scars on his leg and chest that bore witness to the crash and his subsequent surgery. The scar that ran the length of his cheekbone was covered by his hands and the towel. Her face momentarily betrayed the ache in her heart for him that was both love and compassion.

He'd been through hell and now she had the nagging feeling that Hell hadn't finished with him.

She put her hand gently on his shoulder, "Mike?"

He emerged from the towel, eyes red and running and pulled her to him, kissing her firmly on the lips and laughing as she squirmed under his soaking wet embrace.

"You were saying?" he laughed.

"I'm soaking!"

"Yeah, well, if you will come wandering in here when I'm butt naked and soaking wet, poking fun at my agony, you can expect to get wet hugged."

He stopped as he saw the serious look on her face. "Beth?"

"Mike, promise me you'll be careful. I don't like the way things look at the Abbey. Just be careful."

He was immediately glad that he hadn't told her everything. "Hey, it's all right. I'm going back there with Inspector James because I have to, after that, I'll probably forget the Abbey and leave it out of the book."

"You mean it?"

"I promise I'll only go back there if I have to."

She seemed a little mollified and he quickly changed the subject.

"So, you like Jack?" he asked, as he towelled his hair dry.

Beth smiled in genuine pleasure at the thought of Mike's friend. "I think he's lovely. He makes me laugh. I had no idea how close you were. It's such a pity you haven't seen him for a while."

"That doesn't affect Jack and me, we can go for months without catching up, then all of a sudden one of us calls the other and it's like we only spoke the day before."

She smiled, "Good," she whispered. "Martha is quite smitten, says he reminds her of Alex Trefusis, one of her old pupils who she could never quite bring herself to put in detention apparently. Pity he hasn't found the right woman and settled down."

Mike stopped drying his hair and looked at her in surprise. "Are you serious? Found the right man, you mean."

She looked puzzled momentarily, then, "Oh! Oh, I had no idea. Why didn't you tell me?"

Mike shrugged, "It didn't occur to me. Not in the slightest. It's not how I see Jack. To me, he's just Jack and that's all there is to it." He looked at her intently, "It doesn't matter to you, does it? I mean we've never had this conversation before."

"Of course not! It was a surprise that's all. Best not tell Martha, I'm not sure how she'd take it."

"I think she'd surprise you," he said. "Now, hop it and let a man get dressed in peace. The sooner I get out of here, the sooner I'll be back." He put his hands on her shoulders and guided her out of their bathroom, "Back in bed and rest!"

She suddenly felt exhausted and happily settled down under the soft quilt, suddenly conscious of a deep pain in her womb. She held her breath. It went away and didn't return, it was probably Braxton Hicks contractions, her womb practicing for the big event. She relaxed and tried to settle into a doze but her anxiety was getting the better of her.

She tossed and turned for over an hour, then decided to get up and get a coffee and a catch up with Martha. She needed to get her mind away from the Abbey that seemed to be reaching out to her, even though she had never been there. A fact that she was extremely glad of.

CHAPTER TWENTY SIX: THE INN

Mike drove to The Black Mountain Inn faster than he should, he wanted to get this business over with a quickly as possible.

He pulled his car up into the car park and hauled himself out of it, the pain in his leg making him screw up his face. He hesitated and pulled the Tramadol out of his pocket.

He tossed two of the tablets into his mouth and swallowed hard, then strained to hear what he thought was a woman shouting.

"Help! Please, someone help me!"

He began to run awkwardly to the door, ignoring the crescendo of pain that was shooting up his leg. The door to the Inn was closed but gave immediately as he pulled on the latch. It was semi dark inside, none of the curtains had been pulled from the night before.

The scene that met him seemed surreal as he tried to make sense of it.

A woman with peroxide hair stood under the main beam in the hallway holding a man up by his legs. His agile brain quickly processed the information. Geraint had hung himself.

He moved as quickly as he could and grabbed Geraint by the legs.

"Get a knife! Anything!"

Ruby responded immediately and darted for the kitchen, returning straight away with a large carving knife.

"I'll hold him while you cut him down. Go!"

Ruby ran up the ancient staircase to the top landing and reached over the old beam, the hanging beam, and began sawing away at the rope, wincing at the *creak* that the rope made against the ancient oak.

Mike was holding Geraint up against the strain of the rope and suddenly felt the weight give as Ruby cut through it at the beam.

Geraint's face was suffused purple and his eyes were bulging. Mike dropped the landlord heavily onto the floor and bent over him, feeling for a pulse and listening for sounds of breathing. His pulse was weak but steady and his breathing was shallow but there. He was about to tell Ruby to call an ambulance when Geraint suddenly grabbed at his wrist.

"It's okay, you're all right. I'll call an ambulance; you need to go to hospital."

"No," Geraint croaked dryly. "No. Ruby?"

"I'm here Ger! What the hell do you think you were doing, you bloody fool?"

Geraint tried to sit up. "I don't know. I don't know what's happening to me. Ruby, I'm sorry."

"Not as bloody sorry as you will be if you try that sort of stunt again!" she yelled at him.

Mike looked at her, "It's a god job you found him when you did."

She blinked away a few stray tears. "I came in early today 'cause I wanted to see him, quiet like, talk to him about … things."

Mike nodded. "Well, it's a good job you did. Get him some water will you?"

He helped Geraint upright. "You really should go to the hospital you know."

Geraint shook his head. "No."

"Well seeing as how you're being stubborn about it, maybe you'll listen to why I was here this early in the day."

"Didn't take you for an early pint kind of bloke," Geraint said in a hoarse voice. "What do you want from me?"

Mike decided to come straight to the point.

"I'm told you have a certain book. I think you know

the one I mean. I understand it's for sale."

A cloud passed over Geraint's face and his expression became belligerent. "Who told you that? Brian Jenkins, I suppose."

"It doesn't matter, I just want the book, that's all. I expect it has a price?"

Ruby returned from the kitchen, water in hand and a serious expression fixed onto her face. "Just give it to him, Ger. Get rid of the bloody thing. Look what it's done to you."

Geraint looked puzzled. "How do you know about it?"

She shrugged, "I have eyes. I saw it under the bar. I'm not educated or anything but even I could see it looked like a load of trouble. Just give it to him."

Geraint's face fell, "I wish I could, but I can't."

"Why not?" she demanded.

Mike understood immediately. "Because he doesn't have it any more. Am I right?"

Geraint nodded slowly. "I had it here and I was going to sell it today so I thought I'd have a good look at it, see what I could ask for it. But then I came over all queer like, tired and kind of depressed all of a sudden. And cold. Next thing I knew I was holding the rope and then nothing until you cut me down. What's happening to me? I think I may have a brain tumour or something."

Mike put his hand on his shoulder. "I don't think you have a brain tumour. It's more likely the something."

He stood up stiffly, aware of the pain in his leg again. "Believe me; you're better off without it. I don't suppose you can remember anyone coming in here?"

Geraint shook his head. "Unless ... I remember climbing on the bar stool over there, and then I just stepped off it. There was someone. Standing over there by the fireplace. Just watching."

"Did you know who he was?"

"No. It was just a shadow. That's really all I remember."

Mike stared at him long and hard. "So where did you find the book, Geraint?"

He turned his head away from Mike.

"Look at me, man. Where did you find it?"

Tears were pooling in his eyes. "With the old bones," he said, "With the very old bones."

Ruby went white. "Oh my God, Ger, you didn't. Tell me you didn't."

Mike was getting frustrated, "What?" he snapped.

"Geraint Meredith, tell me you didn't dig down in that cellar. Tell me you didn't dig him up. Christ, he was left there 'cause it was always believed to be the safest place. Jesus!"

Geraint turned away again, unable to look her in the face and nodded.

"Will one of you, please tell me what the hell you're talking about!"

Ruby answered him. "Mam told me once that the Black Judge is buried here. Came to his just deserts here, where he did all the hanging and the torturing. Mam said he was buried here, well that's what the locals have always believed anyway."

Mike stood up abruptly and dragged Geraint to his feet. "Show me," he said icily. "Now."

Geraint was shaking, "He's not there. Not anymore."

"What do you mean?"

Geraint suddenly raised his voice to near hysteria, "I mean he's not bloody well there anymore! He was and then he was gone! Someone took him before I could concrete over the old bones. Someone took him and now someone's taken the book!"

Mike clenched his jaws together, twitching the muscles in his cheek. He let go of Geraint who fell back to the floor in a heap, quickly attended by Ruby.

"I have to go, Ruby. Call an ambulance; he needs to get checked out."

Mike was out of the door.

160

CHAPTER TWENTY SEVEN: BACK TO THE ABBEY

It was illogical and irrational but Mike had learned early on to listen to his illogical and irrational instincts. He was heading for the Abbey.

As he pulled his car into the gravelled driveway he immediately noticed the blue and white crime scene tape zig-zagging across the door. He checked his watch. Ten o'clock. He had an hour before Inspector James arrived.

Images of Mary from the previous night and Geraint hanging from the old oak beam at the inn fired his anger. Crime scene tape or not, he was going in. He limped around the building; all doors were similarly adorned. He considered momentarily the possibility of breaking a window then thought better of it. If this was indeed a crime scene, the last thing he wanted or needed was his fingerprints all over the window frame. But he needed to gain entry.

There was something at the back of his mind fighting to come forward. He leaned against a windowsill at the back of the abbey and tried to allow it to take hold.

Looking around him he noticed a small stone building about a hundred yards away, nestling at the edge of a small copse. And there it was; the dusty file had come to the front of his consciousness and he walked as quickly as he could over to the building.

He tried the door and it opened to him at the first attempt. It was a small stone storehouse, about eleven feet by twelve. The dirt floor was covered with old straw and the whole of the interior was dark and gloomy with no windows and no sign of electricity and he'd come unprepared with no flashlight or any of his equipment. But his visit wasn't about recordings and documentation, it was entirely confrontational.

He scanned around the outside and found a large stone which he used to prop open the door and at least allow a minimal amount of daylight. Back inside he began inspecting the floor, stamping hard with his good leg and listening. Eventually the low hollow sound he was listening for filled the building and he began scraping away the straw and loose earth from the area.

In minutes a square of wood appeared. It was there. If his instincts were correct, it was a trap door leading to a tunnel to the abbey connecting with a priest hole. Rarely were these features ever bricked up in modern times, creating interesting stories to be related to visitors and historians. The priest hole was often the saviour of Catholic priests during the Reformation when Catholicism was outlawed and any catholic priest discovered saying mass would be put to death. And this was one such structure. His problem was having no flashlight, and the hundred yards of completely dark tunnel would seem like a mile. If he was going to try it, it had to be now. Inspector James had said eleven o'clock which probably meant he'd be there by quarter to. Forty five minutes was all he had.

Mike prized open the wooden hatch and it came up easily. He knelt down painfully and felt around the inside of the opening until on the opposite side his fingers connected with something wooden. A ladder.

He didn't hesitate, he didn't have the luxury of time to be cautious, and in moments he was climbing painfully down the wooden rungs into inky darkness. At the bottom of the ladder the air was dank and smelled of earth and dampness. Like a grave.

He sensed rather than saw that he was in a very small space and began to feel around him. The earth walls had been shored up with old timbers. He pulled a face. If the tunnel was the same, there would surely have been falls over the centuries, making it impassable or worse, it might fall in on him.

The timbers gave way to stone at one point and as he played his fingers around it, his hand found the opening. It was low to the ground and he wouldn't be able to stand up, but it wasn't so low that he would have to crawl. He thanked all the Gods that he wouldn't have to continue on his knees and then bent low and began the arduous walk towards the abbey.

He had gone about forty yards, blind and in pain, constantly feeling around him, when the walls of the tunnel changed. He stopped to assess what it could mean. Instinctively, he realised that the tunnel was forking in two different directions. Not unusual as large structures such as the abbey would often have more than one priest hole and the two would converged somewhere in their escape tunnel.

He didn't have time for experimentation, he had to choose one of the tunnels and go for it. He chose the left hand opening and continued with no idea how far he had slowly travelled.

After what seemed like an eternity, the floor under his feet began to feel different. The earth floor had given way to timbers and the walls were no longer stone under his fingertips but rough hewn wooden planks. Vegetation had grown between the timbers over the years and were tangled together effectively narrowing the tunnel. And from the ache in his leg, he knew that the tunnel was rising in a steady gradient. It was a good sign, it probably meant that he was inside the abbey and the tunnel was soon to emerge within the upstairs of the building.

He carried on with less caution and suddenly tripped forwards over something heavy on the ground. He felt his cheek graze and his titanium knee got a hefty jolt which made him yell out in pain.

"Shit!"

He picked himself up gingerly and brushed himself down, spitting dirt and stray bits of gravel from his mouth, and then carefully felt around the floor to find what he had tripped over and to see if he could feel any more obstacles. His hands found a bone. Then another. He carefully ran his fingers over the floor and took a step back as he identified skeletal remains. In the pitch blackness he felt gently around the rib cage and his fingers traced the outline of a large cross on a heavy chain. The escape tunnel of the priest had become his grave. He lifted the cross from the skeleton and put it into his pocket to give to Radford later.

There was nothing else on the floor so he carried on.

He was suddenly aware that the air around him had changed, it was warmer and the smell of wet earth had vanished. He was surely within the abbey. He reached ahead of him and carried on walking until his hands told him that he had come to the end of the tunnel. There was no ladder this time, but a set of ancient wooden steps that led up to … nothing.

"Ah crap." He felt around the walls and realised that he was standing in a space little bigger than he was. He felt the walls and quickly understood that they were plastered. All except a narrow strip of ancient wood, about five feet high and two and a half feet wide. He leaned against it and pushed. It didn't move.

He pushed harder. It still didn't move. He leaned against it, thinking rapidly. His options were non-existent. If he couldn't exit the tunnel he would have to go back the way he'd come. He didn't have time to try the other tunnel and he was exhausted. He stepped away from the wooden strip and leaned against the top of it, thinking. It swung outwards, the bottom connecting painfully with his good shin.

From the other side, it was a vertical oak beam set in the wall, it was in fact on a pivot, so as he had leaned against the whole thing in the middle it hadn't budged, but pressure against the top had swung it open on its fulcrum into a horizontal position. The opening was very narrow and now he had no choice but to get down onto his knees and crawl painfully through the opening into the abbey.

As he had suspected he had emerged into an upstairs room and he quickly made for the door. He was at the far end of the upstairs landing, at the top of the stairs.

"Judge Thomas Llewellyn! Show yourself! Or is it helpless young girls you prefer! Show yourself to me! Or get back to the stinking reaches of Hell where you came from."

He heard his own words that had come out of his mouth unexpectedly and at high volume and he cringed. He had no means of taking on the evil that he was calling on, and no quick exit either.

Bloody idiot. What in God's name do you think you're doing? Breaking every rule in the goddamn book and then some, that's what. But Mary ... I'm not going to stand for that!

As his thoughts were racing across the synapses in his brain, he suddenly felt a draft. He spun around and saw the blue grey shape at the stair head. This time it stopped in front of him, and he felt himself become disorientated and nauseous as the shadow engulfed him. Something hit him hard behind his knees and as he fell to the floor a heavy object connected with the back of his skull. And as he lost consciousness, the whispers began.

CHAPTER TWENTY EIGHT:
PARANORMAL ACTIVITY

"He's coming. He's coming for the childe. Protect the childe. He's coming …"

"Eleanor, I hath no right to forgiveness, but I beseech thee, forgive me. Our childe …"

"He's coming. He's coming for the childe. Protect the childe."

"Eleanor …"

The whispering faded into the fabric of the abbey as Mike groaned and opened his eyes. He struggled to focus on the image that was swimming above him. It coalesced into a face and he tried to sit up too quickly. His fist shot out and connected with air as the face retreated before he could make contact.

"Travis, what the hell are you doing in here? And how did you get here? This is very serious and I should arrest you for entering a crime scene. What happened to you?"

Mike grimaced. "Nothing that will stand up in court."

Inspector James's face stopped veering in and out of focus and steadied itself above him as the policeman lifted Mike to his feet. "You'd better do some explaining. Come downstairs to the library. Can you walk?"

Mike pulled another face. "After a fashion."

Inspector James went on ahead of him, turning to check Mike was behind him twice. In the library he sat at the desk and indicated a chair opposite. Mike sat.

"Now, I want to know how you gained entry to this place when I had to cut through the crime scene tape to get in. And I want an explanation as to why. And it had better be good."

"First tell me how Mary is."

167

"As I understand it from the hospital her mind has completely retreated somewhere that it can't be reached. It may be permanent."

Mike ground his teeth and inhaled deeply. His fists were balled at his side.

"So, perhaps you'd be good enough to answer my questions."

Mike told him about finding Geraint and Ruby.

"So you left another potential crime scene. Not good." He shook his head.

"Look, Inspector, I know you probably think this is all nonsense but …"

"But no probably about it. A girl has been molested and the only other person present was you. Now you tell me a man has tried to hang himself, or perhaps he had some help? Mm? You were there again. And if you try to tell me one more time that it was the ghost of some long dead judge, then I'm afraid I'll be taking you in. So try and come up with the truth?"

Mike slammed his fist into the desk. "I'm telling you the truth. You've seen the video tape. And when you brought my laptop back last night you said you didn't understand any of it and that your guys had found no editing. If you think I'm guilty why bring back the evidence?"

"What evidence? Just because we can't find any tinkering with the recording doesn't mean you didn't. In fact, I'm inclined to take you in anyway. Unless you can convince me in the next five minutes to the contrary. Start by telling me how you got in here."

Mike told him about the priest hole and the tunnel.

"Okay, that's the how, in itself a crime, entering a crime scene is an offence. Now for the why."

Mike sighed and dragged his fingers through his hair that was liberally sprinkled with dust and dirt particles from the tunnel, flinching as his fingers connected with something sticky. He began the lengthy explanation about his investigation and how he believed it was connected to what had happened at the Black Mountain Inn.

"So, let me get this straight. You believe that the body of Sir Thomas Llewellyn had been buried in the cellar of the inn, along with some iffy book and they have somehow 'influenced' the landlord. But now they aren't there. And you thought they would be here. So you came here to try and prove your theory. Concealing the burial of a body is an offence."

"Oh come on! The bastard was topped and buried in sixteen fifty four! I'd like to know how you think I was responsible for concealing that! I haven't yet mastered time travel!"

"Flippancy won't get you anywhere, Travis. You should have called us when you discovered it."

"You're not listening! I told you; neither the bones of the old bastard nor his damn book are there now. So what was there to call you about?"

"So why did you come here?"

Mike was exasperated and pushed his chair back and stood up.

"Sit down."

Mike leaned on the table. "If you're going to arrest me, then do it. My lawyer will have me out in minutes. You've got nothing."

"Got a local lawyer, have you? I understood you only moved here from London a few days ago."

Mike eyed him carefully; the guy had obviously done his homework and was more than interested in him. He tried another tactic.

"Okay, I'm sorry, but I'm telling you the truth. I can't do any more than that."

The inspector was quiet, fiddling with his pen and staring at the desk top. He appeared to come to a decision.

"It'll probably cost me my pension, but for some reason which is beyond me, I think I believe you. So do you think that this … spirit is any threat to anyone else?"

169

"I honestly don't know. If I understand it correctly, he has been brought back into the earthly plane by means of black magic and has preyed on Mary, using sexual energy to feed on and build up his own energy. Sick as it sounds, that is what I believe is the truth. Such spirits are common in literature and other documents. They're known as an incubus. You can look it up in any decent dictionary. As to his further intentions, I have no idea, but I do think that he isn't done yet."

A sudden loud bang from the hallway had them both on their feet. It was followed by a loud high pitched keening noise that made them both cover their ears. It was followed by a howling wind that seemed to start at the top of the stairs and was tilting pictures on the walls as it came closer. In the hallway they struggled to keep their feet against the force of the wind that had come from nowhere. Inspector James had his hand out in front of his ashen face. Their jackets were whipped backwards and they were losing the fight to remain upright. The shrill keening noise reached a crescendo and their eardrums responded in agony.

Mike was suddenly flung against the wall, the breath being knocked out of him as he hit it. Lights were flicking on and off and doors were opening of their own volition and slamming shut in the same manner. The chandelier above their heads was swaying wildly and the accompanying creaking noise announced its parting company with its fixing. In a heartbeat it was descending above the inspectors head.

"Move!" shouted Mike.

The inspector looked up and threw himself out of its path as it crashed to the floor sending shards of crystal everywhere. He was white and shaking as he grabbed his phone from his pocket.

"Get out!" Mike shouted. "For God's sake get out!"

They fought against the howling wind and made it to the front door. It took the strength of both of them to heave it open and they fell out into the morning sunlight, breathing painfully and staggering forwards as the door slammed shut behind them.

"Are you all right, Inspector?" Mike gasped.

"Jim," he said breathlessly, "Call me Jim. What in God's name happened?"

"Not in God's name. Whatever is in there has nothing to do with him."

Jim James shook his head, his mouth wide open but no words would form on his tongue. He leaned against his car fighting for his breath. Mike slapped his pocket and realised he had left his phone in the car.

Jim James gasped, "Jesus Christ. And you do this for a living? Go home. I'll be in touch."

CHAPTER TWENTY NINE: LABOUR

Beth and Martha were sitting in the sunlit sitting room sipping strong coffee. Beth shifted her position trying to get comfortable as the pain in her temple shot lightning bolts into her head, making her squeeze her eyes shut and her hand to fly to her forehead.

"What?" demanded Martha.

"It's nothing; it's just this pain I keep getting. Martha, there's a ... spirit in the cottage. Her name is Adain and whenever she's around it's as if she tries to get my attention this way."

Martha's eyes were hawk-like and she remained silent.

Beth began to weep quietly.

Martha said nothing but sat next to her and hesitantly put her arm around her as Beth recounted the events that had brought her to the conclusion.

"Seems like you two attract this sort of thing. Nothing you can't deal with between you."

"I know, it's just that ... argh!" She doubled up at the pain.

Martha was on her feet instantly. "Put your feet up, where's the pain?"

Beth put her hand over her belly.

"First one?" Martha quizzed her. Beth shook her head.

"How many?"

"A few. Do you think ...?"

"I think it's time we called your midwife. Where's her number?"

"In the kitchen next to the kettle. Aaargh!"

Despite her bulk, Martha was swiftly in the kitchen and returned instantly with the card that Kath had left. "Phone?" she demanded.

Beth pointed to her writing desk and Martha was instantly dialling the number.

When she put the phone down she turned to Beth, "She's on her way. Five minutes. Get you some water."

"No, I'm ... Aaargh!"

"I'm no midwife child, but these pains are coming too quickly for my liking. Maybe I should call an ambulance."

"No, Martha, don't. I'll feel better with Kath, at least I kind of know her. Please wait."

"Boil water. That's what they say. Plenty of boiling water." She hurried back to the kitchen and Beth heard her filling the kettle and several saucepans.

"Give me the phone, Martha. I want to call Mike. I want him with me."

Before Martha could oblige the doorbell rang and she hurried to answer it. She returned with Kath Dickinson.

"Right then, Beth, looks like we're getting the show on the road. Let me have a look at you." She busied herself with listening to the baby's heartbeat and then took Beth's blood pressure.

"I need to examine you," she said nodding meaningfully at Martha who took the hint and disappeared back to the kitchen.

Minutes later Kath joined her. "She's in labour all right, and it's progressing too quickly. I've given her a sedative to slow things down a bit. Her blood pressure is way too high. I'm taking her straight to the maternity unit, no time to wait for hubby. Perhaps you can contact him and get him to meet us there. Looks like she's going to be a mum today."

Martha nodded at her. "I'll come too."

Kath frowned. "Sorry, I've only a two seater. Are you a relative?"

"I'm a friend. A close friend."

"Usually only husbands and partners in the delivery suite I'm afraid. Maybe you can get things ready for when I bring her back later?"

She didn't wait for Martha's reply and was helping Beth out of the door before she could argue.

"My phone is on the sofa, Martha. Keep calling Mike for me."

Martha nodded as the two of them disappeared out of the door.

She found Mike's number on Beth's contact list and dialled. It rang unanswered and went through to his voicemail.

"Michael. It's Martha. Call me."

She realised how the message would panic him and dialled again. "Beth's in labour Michael, but the midwife has been and she's taken her to the hospital. Call me."

Then she turned abruptly and went to the window. A movement in the far right of the garden caught her eye. The woman stood staring back at here.

Martha stomped outside as the woman walked towards her, though 'walked' was the wrong use of the verb as the woman appeared to glide towards her.

Martha was unphased and stood her ground.

"I expect you're the one causing problems to my friend. Well, I won't tolerate it. Bugger off."

The woman stood directly in front of her, head on one side a quizzical expression on her face. She spoke but the words went unheard.

"Look, I can't hear you. I told you. Bugger off."

The woman reached out towards Martha and laid a hand on her arm. Martha felt a tingle where the woman's hand appeared and as the spectral figure spoke again, Martha heard the words settle in her consciousness. She listened carefully, nodded briefly then hurried upstairs to her boxes.

She ripped one of them open unceremoniously and rummaged through the books inside, plucking one out and sitting down on the bed, leafing through its pages.

She was lost in several books by the time the phone rang again.

"Hello? Michael. Good."

"Martha! What's happening? Where's Beth?"

"She's gone into labour. Midwife took her to the maternity unit. But Michael, I'm worried."

"Which hospital? Abergavenny or Hereford?"

"Abergavenny."

"Right, that will be Nevill Hall hospital then. I'm on my way and I have to pass by home, I need to change before I go. I'll call the hospital; call me if you hear from her."

"Michael…" The line went dead.

Martha frowned. She was deeply worried.

Seconds later Beth's telephone shrilled it's tune again.

"Hello?"

"Martha! I called both hospitals and they said they didn't know anything about Beth. She's not on any of their records. And they don't know any Kath Dickinson! Where is she? Christ almighty, you were supposed to be watching her! Who came for her?"

For the first time she could remember, Martha felt helpless.

"Michael, I'm sorry. Beth gave me her number. She said she was her midwife, I had no idea. Though I've a better idea now. You need to go back to the Abbey, lad."

"I'll be home in a couple of minutes." He disconnected.

He slammed his foot onto the accelerator then slowed again and pulled over, grabbing his phone and dialling.

Jim James's phone went straight through to voicemail. He tried again. Same result.

He sat back into his seat, thinking fast. Then he dialled again.

"Jack? It's me. I need your help, big time. I don't have time to explain but I need you to bring a chopper *now*. Hover over the garden and haul me in, I'll explain when you get here."

The panic in his voice was explanation enough. Jack ended his conversation abruptly with his potential client and showed him the door. Friends were friends. Business was just business.

Three minutes later he had cleared take off with air traffic control and was heading north-east for Monmouth. He had no clearance for landing and he knew his license was on the line but he also knew from Mike's voice that he was in trouble.

"Martha!" Mike yelled from the doorway.

"Mike. God help me, I didn't know. Though I should have."

Mike hugged her. "It's not your fault. It's mine. I should have been here. Tell me what happened."

Martha cleared the unfamiliar emotion from her throat and concisely told him what had taken place.

"I saw the woman, Mike. In the garden. She tried to talk to me and I couldn't hear. I tried to dismiss her but she touched me and I understood. Instantly. I understood."

"Then explain it to me," he said in a voice no more than a whisper.

"They want a child to baptise in the name of the devil. They want a life to give in order to allow Astaroth entry to this world. I heard the words, 'A life for a life'. I don't know why her. But I know they intend to use the evil surrounding someone called Thomas Llewellyn. They need a book which contains the ritual and Adain told me that they have it."

"They do now." His jaw was clamped shut and the muscle working in his cheek seemed to underline his scar.

"I know where to go. God help me, maybe it's because I went there and provoked some sleeping entity. If I hadn't …"

"You do what you do. Someone has to stand up to spiritual evil. You do it well."

"But Beth … and the baby."

"Beth is part of it. Part of you. Always will be. I'm coming with you."

He shook his head. "No. Jack will be here in a minute, I need you to stay here."

Before she could reply the thunder of the rotor blades of Jack's helicopter brought conversation to an end and Mike was out of the door fighting against the downdraft from the blades. Jack had thrown out the emergency ladder and Mike was hauling himself inside as Martha pulled on her coat to carry out the last of Adain's advice.

She found Old Brookstone farm at the end of the lane opposite the church. She banged on the peeling paint of the old front door and was answered by a tall, spare woman, with iron grey hair pulled tightly into a knot at the nape of her neck. She wore a long skirt and welsh woollen shawl draped her shoulders.

"I'm told you're the person I need to speak with," said Martha.

The woman fixed her with intelligent coal black eyes. "You'd better come in.

CHAPTER THIRTY: DARK MAGIC

Mike had updated Jack on the short flight that had saved him the best part of an hour in the car. Jack's face was grey as he landed the helicopter in the ample space in front of the Abbey.

"They're gonna know you're here, Spooky."

"They will soon enough anyway," Mike snarled.

Mike was out and on the ground before the rotors had come to a halt. He bent low and was heading for the door before Jack could catch up with him.

"Mike! Wait!" His muscular legs caught up with his friend and Jack grabbed his shoulder. "At least wait for me."

The door was framed in blue and white tape hanging loose where Jim James had cut into it. Mike pushed the door. It was heavier than he remembered but it opened into the dark hallway as he put his weight behind it.

Shattered crystal still strewed the floor of the hallway and there was a cold chill that seeped into his bones. He shivered and started as Jack came up behind him and laid a hand on his shoulder.

"Shit! Don't do that, Jack!"

"What the hell happened here? Why is it so bloody cold?"

They could see their breath forming mists in front of them. The abbey was quiet. Too quiet. Maybe he was wrong, maybe they hadn't taken Beth there after all. And he didn't know who 'they' were. Perhaps he'd been arrogant in believing that he knew what was happening and where Beth was. He felt a rising panic, if he was in the wrong place …

A muffled thump came to them from upstairs. Mike

179

was ahead of Jack who was still bewildered by what was unfolding, when a tortured scream galvanised him into movement and he was at the top of the stairs before Mike.

They stood on the landing listening for more sound that would give them a direction. Jack was shivering uncontrollably and his teeth were chattering as the temperature plummeted even further.

A blue grey mist was forming and the whispering echoed around them, so quiet at first they could hardly discern the words and then as another scream rent the air the whispers were all around them.

"He's coming. He's coming for the childe. Protect the childe."

"You should get out," said Mike is a forced whisper. "This isn't your fight, I called you to get me here quickly, and that's all. Get out while you can."

Jack's face was a picture of fear. "No chance. I'm in it now, for good or ill. I'm coming with you." He hadn't abandoned his friend in Afghanistan and he had no intention of doing so now.

Another blood curdling scream propelled Mike towards the door at the end of the corridor.

"Beth!"

The wooden bar and bolt were gone and there was an icy covering on the outside of the door. The door was so cold it burned into Mike's flesh as he pushed it open. The smell that hit them made Jack retch and stagger backwards.

"God in Heaven!"

A deep guttural laugh made their skin crawl off their bones. Jack grabbed Mike.

"Mike? What the Hell is that? What are you going to do? We're unarmed, we haven't thought this through!" His panic was obvious.

"No time," was all Mike could say. He was through the door and Jack was inches behind him, still shivering and shaking. Mike seemed in control, focussed only on Beth and he took some strength from it.

The door opened into a huge room with no sign of

rotting floorboards and timbers.

The walls of the room were panelled to waist height with grotesque carvings of all manner of imagery from the Pit. Twisted and grotesque faces leered out from the oak panelling above which the walls were painted a red hue that was so dark it was almost black. There were painted demonic sigils on every wall. The floor was marble tiled and centrally was incorporated in red tiles, the inverted pentagram inside a circle, the pentagram contained the head of a goat. Central to the room was a large ornate altar on which lay a writhing, agonised, Beth. Around the altar was a circle of fire, fed by oil in a circular channel ten feet in diameter and surrounding the whole structure.

Mike's head span as he lunged forwards towards her, unthinking, uncaring of the two figures that were bearing down on him.

"Welcome, we have been expecting you."

He spun around in time to see the black robed figure of Gavin St John Radford lift his arm and point at his chest. He felt the pain as it seared beneath his ribs and he fell to his knees, sending flames of pain through his entire leg. He gasped and hung his head at his own stupidity. If nothing else, Crowsmoor should have taught him not to underestimate the dark power that black magicians could harness when trained to the ultimate degree, regardless of the cost to their immortal souls. Radford was obviously an adept of a high degree because in that one simple motion he had rendered Mike immobile and struck dumb.

Jack was sprawled on the floor beside him, unmoving.

The scream that formed in his brain found no voice and emerged from him in a stream of hot tears. He had brought her to this.

Radford laughed aloud as he read his thoughts.

"You fool! Don't credit yourself with any of this; you were just a tool of my master. It is I that summoned you when I learned of her. There is a perfect symmetry to it, the vessel of the child that shall become the daughter of

Astaroth once a servant of a pitiful God. The child will be born into darkness and there she shall live, brought up to revere my master and eventually serve him as a true vessel for his own child."

Mike fought to stand but Radford's eyes were wide and penetrating, sending waves of icy blackness that reached into his soul.

"It is good that you are here to witness what shall be done, your emotions will only serve to feed Astaroth and enhance his manifestation."

Mike was suddenly aware of the other figure as she sidled naked towards Radford. Kath Dickinson, who he knew only as Mrs Evans, tilted her head on one side in a mocking gesture that brought thoughts of murder to the forefront of his consciousness.

"That's right, good, the more you suffer and conjure those emotions, the better it will be for Astaroth. You can do nothing but witness the birth of his daughter."

My daughter! The unspoken words careered around his brain, echoing into eternity.

Kath Dickinson draped her nudity around Radford laughing and whispered into his ear. He nodded at her.

"Pain too, will help to bring him and it seems that my companion enjoys pain, pain in others that is. So …"

He began an incantation that had to originate in the depths of Hell, his eyes ablaze with unholy fire.

Mike braced himself for the blast that would surely come from his outstretched hand, but it didn't come. Instead Radford lowered his voice and began talking in a hypnotic tone.

"Your poor useless leg. Better to have stayed dead in the wreckage of your helicopter than to live like this, a cripple who can't protect the woman he loves. Feel the pain, feel it burning into your soul, you pitiful excuse of a man. The metal inside you is but clay in my hand. See?"

He made a twisting motion with his hand and Mike felt the titanium rod in his lower leg respond, mirroring

Radford's gesture. The agony etched on his face made Radford smile. He gestured to Mike's knee and repeated the twisting movement of his hand.

The excruciating pain as his knee joint dislocated made him want to vomit, he felt the bile rise in his throat all the while he kept his eyes fixed on Beth who continued to writhe in the agony of imminent birth.

Kath Dickinson crossed to the altar and hauled Beth's feet into stirrups at the end of the altar and Mike fought the rising faint.

"Give her something, it's not time yet," snapped Radford, and Kath responded with a hypodermic syringe into Beth's arm. It seemed to quiet her and for that Mike was grateful, his agony forgotten as his mind shifted a gear, desperate to calm himself and bring rational thought back into focus and be able to ignore Radford's taunts. No emotion. No response.

Radford had positioned himself in front of the altar with Kath Dickinson opposite, writhing against the altar and in a state of obvious arousal. Mike spat onto the floor in disgust.

The temperature fell another degree as Gavin opened an old leather bound book and began the infernal incantations.

He called on Satan Lord of Darkness, and bowed in all four directions to Lucifer, Belial, Leviathan and Astaroth.

Beth cried out and Kath switched over into midwife mode to delivery her baby. Mike fought to keep his focus; he was biting the inside of his cheek and could taste the coppery taint of his own blood. He would be no good to her if he lost it.

Gavin continued his invocation to Astaroth, all the while tracing diagrams from the book in the air.

"Astaroth, I invoke Thee
Astaroth I summon Thee
Astaroth I conjure Thee

Come forth Astaroth and manifest Thyself
In this body which has been prepared for Thee
Come forth Astaroth and manifest Thyself
Open the fifth lock of the Abyss Astaroth
Come forth Astaroth and manifest thyself
Come forth Astaroth and manifest thyself."

He made the sign of the demon in the air with a ritual knife.

The sight of the ritual knife galvanised Mike's thought processes. If only he could break the psychic attack from Gavin. *Stop thinking, stop fighting, it just makes the hold stronger.* His mind went back to Crowsmoor.

Mike closed his eyes and invoking the Lords of Light, he prayed.

There was no blinding flash of light or shattering of windows this time. Nothing seemed to have changed. He tried again, summoning all of his strength and will. Nothing changed.

His concentration was broken again. This time it was the cry of a new-born child. His new-born child. His tears stung as they made hot rivulets down his cheek. *Not here. Not like this.*

CHAPTER THIRTY ONE: THE LORDS OF LIGHT

Mike couldn't even look away as Gavin deftly cut through the baby's umbilical cord with the ritual knife. Beth was scarily quiet and he thought he was going to throw up.

Directly in front of the altar in the middle of the remains of Thomas Llewellyn a plume of grey smoke was forming. It swirled and spiralled into a tall column six feet high. He closed his eyes and continued to call the Lords of Light, visualising white light but again his concentration was ripped away as Gavin held out his hands and Kath laid the infant in them.

Dear God no! Please, no! His voice was impotent, heard only in his own head.

He hung his head, Radford was right; he *was* a pathetic excuse for a man, unable to protect his own loved ones. He felt as if he was choking.

The column of smoke was thinning and he could just make out the shape of a man. Slowly the smoke diminished and was replaced by an eerie blue glow.

Astaroth was manifesting.

He was using the old bones as a focus for the manifestation. In essence it was a possession of the remains of the lecherous judge; a fitting foul receptacle for a filthy emanation from the Pit.

From previous studies Mike knew that the demon Astaroth had a hideous appearance; ugly and winged, he rode a dragon and carried a viper in his hand, he was summoned to guide people to hidden treasure and to answer their questions. His mind went back to De Montefort's journal. He had written that he had hidden treasure 'within these very walls'. Jesus Christ, this was all

185

about finding lost treasure? His murderous thoughts took hold of him again as he watched, helpless, as Radford used the child's own blood, still adorning her face, to sign her with an upside down pentagram on her forehead.

"I baptise thee in the name of Lord Satan, child of darkness, and give thee as a gift to Astaroth. *Astaroth!*" His voice reached a crescendo and became frenzied as he called the name 'Astaroth!' again and again. And again.

The Satanist took the birth blood that had pooled onto the table and flung it hard onto the skeletal remains of Judge Llewellyn and stood transfixed.

"A life for a life!" he screamed.

A tall man stepped out of the blue light, wearing tight black leather trousers and boots, bare chest revealing rippling musculature and a perfectly defined body. The old bones were no longer on the floor.

His hair was blacker than night and it matched the dense anthracite eyes. His arched eyebrows framed a cruel countenance that had no right to be as handsome as it was. His sensual lips formed a smile as he stepped forwards. Not ugly, no wings, no dragon and no viper.

Kath Dickinson slinked towards him, offering herself. There was nothing to do now, but pray for their souls.

Astaroth's cruel mouth twisted into the parody of a smile and there was lust in the coal black eyes. He allowed Kath to move in close to him. She lifted her left leg and wrapped it around the demon, pressing her naked body against him.

He gave a cruel laugh and flung her backwards.

"See to the woman," he snarled.

Realisation hit Mike like a thunderbolt, and hung his head in desperation. Hung his head. Movement was returning. He daren't give it away; he had to wait for the right moment. He flexed his toes inside his shoes. Yes! He tried to make tiny movements to confirm it but whilst his muscles were contracting, there was only the slightest movement. Only a matter of time. If he had it.

Radford was relaxing his hold on him. The psychic attack was losing its grip on him whilst his attention was elsewhere.

Jack was stirring and pushed himself upright. Astaroth tipped his head on one side and the cruel mouth became a lascivious smile. He crossed to Jack in three strides and hauled him roughly to his feet appraising him carefully. The terror on Jack's face painted its own picture as he assimilated the scene before him.

Astaroth's penetrating anthracite eyes fixed him as he entered his mind.

Mike tried to move, there was slightly more response from his brain and his muscles but still not enough to get to his feet.

Jack was staring into the terrifyingly beautiful eyes.

Jack! Don't look at him. Turn away! Mike willed his friend.

But Jack wasn't looking away.

The mask of terror had relaxed as he stood stock still in front of the demon.

Astaroth raised his hand and very slowly dragged a long fingernail down Jack's face, neck and onto his chest. Jack smiled.

No, No, Dear God in Heaven, no!

The demon's voice seemed to fill the room, yet it was low and seductive. It echoed in Mike's brain like an obscenity.

He looked Jack up and down once more. "Now this is more like it." The seduction had begun.

Astaroth pulled Jack towards him and was against him in an instant. Before Mike shut his eyes to pray for a swift end to the torture, he was left with the image of Astaroth kissing Jack on the mouth. And Jack was responding, one arm around the demon, his other hand unbuttoning his shirt and pulling it wide open. And pushing himself deeper into Astaroth's writhing embrace.

If there was Hell on Earth, this was it and Mike was in it and teetering on the edge of the abyss of madness.

The minutes that followed were surreal, of a dreamlike quality. This was it. Mike knew he had lost his grip on sanity.

The door to the temple suddenly crashed open and Martha, Mam Thomas, Dai Bricks and Jim James entered the obscene temple. It was a nightmare that they had no place in. He shook his head trying to understand.

He felt a simultaneous release of the attack on him and was on his feet and throwing his body towards Beth, not noticing that with the release of the psychic attack, his leg was not twisted and his knee not dislocated. Such was the power of Radford's influence on the mind. His focus was purely on Beth.

Jack had his arms around Astaroth and was allowing the vile creature from the Pit to lick his neck and thrust his tongue into his mouth.

Surreal turned to chaos and two terrible screams ripped through the temple.

Beth stirred on the altar, as Martha snatched the wailing infant from Gavin Radford. Mike grabbed the ritual knife that clattered to the floor, but before he could ram it into Radford's chest a heavy fist had taken the Satanist to the floor and a pair of tired looking shoes were kicking him repeatedly and hard. He wasn't getting up any time soon.

Jim James scowled at the unconscious form under his foot. He didn't caution him or read him his rights. He just had.

"Beth!" Mike flung himself at her, lifting her up from the altar. He shook her, calling her name. There was no response. Terrified he felt for a pulse and could feel nothing as she lay cold against his arms like a rag doll.

A foul odour was filling the room, he spun around.

Jack was standing facing him, pale and shaking in front of a black gelatinous mess oozing over some very old bones, the source of the stench. And in the middle of the stinking black slime lay his gold locket, now empty of the consecrated communion wafer that his mother had given to him years ago for his protection, its purpose fulfilled. In the middle of the embraces from Astaroth, as he unbuttoned his shirt, he had yanked it roughly from around his neck, breaking the chain and had shoved the wafer violently into the throat of the demon.

Martha held the infant close to her ample chest, safe inside her tweed jacket.

He didn't know which way to turn, his child or Beth?

A scratchy laugh brought him to face Kath Dickinson being held roughly, arms pulled behind her, by Dai Bricks. "She's dying," she spat. "She has no further use!"

His grief and rage and torture exited from him in a whirlwind of agony as he flew towards her, when he was suddenly grabbed from behind.

"Oh no, you don't! You don't want that kind of stain on your soul. Leave her to me." Mike fought against Jim James who held him tight. "It's enough what will be done. Go to your wife."

Mike bent over Beth, cradling her in his arms, stroking her face, his tears wetting her cheek, when he felt an almost imperceptible breath. His fingers flew to her throat; there was a faint movement under them, and then nothing.

"Someone call an ambulance!" he yelled as he tried to lift Beth from the altar.

The tall, spare woman with the iron grey hair was at his side, a restraining hand on his arm. He lifted his arm to throw her off.

"No. You need to listen to me, to trust me. There isn't much time. She's lost. On the astral planes between life and death. The rituals and the drugs they gave her have seen to that. Hospitals can do nothing for her, but you can.

Mike too was lost. He stared at her uncomprehendingly.

"You called on the Lords of Light. They have answered. They always do, though not always in bursts of light and flame. Sometimes they use a more human response."

189

Mike looked at Martha, Dai Bricks and Mam Thomas. He didn't understand yet, but he knew one thing, he would do whatever it took to save Beth.

Martha held the baby out to him.

Mam Thomas nodded briefly. "One minute is all you have. You have to go onto the astral, near death yourself, to reclaim her and bring her back. I have the means."

"I let her down. I couldn't help her. God help me, I couldn't fight him."

"The Lords of Light heard you. They answered you. *Now* is the time for you to do your part. You have to die, or be as near to death as will take you onto the astral plane. There you must look for her. But you must know this before you go. There will be dark entities on that level of the astral, and when you find her, you have to remember, she has the choice whether to return or not. The Lords of Light have answered you and so they will offer a certain amount of protection but it will mostly be down to you."

Mike nodded and stepped forwards to take his baby into his arms.

She was beautiful, with Beth's eyes. Martha had wiped away the foul symbol on her forehead and had wrapped her in her own jacket. He bent over her and kissed her on top of her head as his heart felt about to explode out of his chest in a volley of intense love and fear.

"I'm leaving you with your Aunt Martha for a little while, angel. I have to go find Mummy."

He turned to Martha who was unashamedly weeping and passed the baby back to her. His voice was gravel. "Take her away from here."

CHAPTER THIRTY TWO: NEAR DEATH

Martha nodded and turned on her heel to do his bidding as Jim James's foot connected heavily again with Gavin Radford as he stirred.

"That's for young Mary," he murmured. He bent to handcuff him.

Dai Bricks tightened his hold on Kath making her squeal in pain. "No need for that, see. Leave them here, locked in look. They'll be dealt with better than you could even dream of. There's other laws at work in this old universe than man's laws, isn't it?"

He stared at Jim and nodded. "I'm telling you, boy. There's nothing that you could do to them compared to what their so called master will. Failed him, they have. Not going to like that, see?"

The Inspector was quiet but his mind was working at lightning speed. He was and always would be a copper, dedicated to bringing evil doers to book but the previous twenty four hours had opened his mind to evil doers that did not inhabit a physical body. At the very least Gavin St John Radford was guilty of kidnapping and possibly murder. Kath Dickinson was obviously an accomplice and guilty of assault. He considered the due process of the law, the deadly slow pace at which the wheels of the law turned and glib lawyers who could get Jack the Ripper off on a technicality. He nodded his understanding and agreement.

"Better get from here then."

His fist flew up and knocked Kath Dickinson out cold. "Throw her down there with that other tosser."

Dai Bricks obliged silently, nodded to Mam Thomas and left with Jim James.

Mike put his hand on Jack's arm. "You okay?"

191

Jack was obviously far from okay and was still visibly shaking. "I'm sorry, Spooky. It's all I could think of. I let him …" He swallowed. "I let him do that so I could get close to him. I don't know where it came from, but I suddenly knew what I had to do. I'm so sorry you had to see that."

He raised his hand. "Don't," he said gently. "I know Jack. Will you go and take care of Martha and the baby, take them away from here. There's something I have to do."

Jack went even whiter. "Mike, do you know what you're doing? I mean … shit, I don't know *what* I mean, but can you trust that woman?"

He looked his friend directly in his eyes. "I have to, Jack. I have to try. Beth's lost. And I'm going to find her. Just do as I ask. Please."

Jack hesitated.

"Please, Jack. And if I don't come back …"

Jack threw his hand up in the air, shaking his head, unwilling to go there. "Just fucking well come back."

His emotions were too much and he turned to leave his friend with Mam Thomas. He turned back momentarily, "Keys are in the whirly bird, help yourself. I'm going back with the old feller and Martha. But I don't like it!"

Mam Thomas's voice cut through the emotion of the moment. "Pick her up, lad. Let's get her out of this place."

Mike obeyed her; Beth was light, too light, in his arms. They took her out of the temple and he limped along the galleried landing towards one of the bedrooms. He laid her gently on the bed as he heard the steady thuds of Jim James nailing the door to the temple shut.

He felt at her throat for her pulse again. For many seconds there was nothing and then he felt a movement, a flutter, and it was gone again.

Mam Thomas held two tiny glass vials of a muddy brown liquid. She gave one to him.

"It's Atropa Belladonna, Deadly Nightshade. Ten

drops will kill you. And Fly Agaric which gives access to the deeper dimensions of the dead. It's a dangerous gateway that you are crossing here."

"I take it there's less than ten drops?"

"Nine. You have to be at the point of death to be able to reach her."

"It's nowhere I've not been before."

"I think you'll find that it is."

"What's the other one for?"

"I'm coming with you."

"What??? No!"

"Listen to me. There are several gates to pass through and the lower astral is home to many things, some good, most not. There are entities roaming the astral, most of them are of a low intellect and of unpleasant appearance. Best to just ignore them. Give them attention and they'll feed on it and grow."

"How do you know these things?"

"Explanations later. Right now, Beth is lost on the astral plane, but if she crosses over onto a higher plane, there will be no coming back. That's why time is vital. Are you going, or not?"

Mike pulled the cork from the glass vial and swallowed the foul tasting liquid then went to lie on the bed next to Beth as Mam Thomas sat in a chair. He was already feeling the effects of the poison.

Their journey had begun.

* * * *

It was dark. And he was cold. He was very cold.

There was a voice in his head, in the higher frequencies of his hearing. He looked around for the source and felt rather saw Mam Thomas at his side.

'There is no need of vocal cords on the astral planes. You hear my thoughts and I hear yours. You doubt yourself. That cannot be. Doubt is a negative emotion and will attract all manner of low

creatures and dark entities. Curb your fears as they will hinder your progress.'

'I'm not afraid. Where will I find her? Tell me.'

'We have to pass through the first gate. It will be lighter then.'

'I don't remember this. Last time I mean. It wasn't dark.'

'It's different this time. You have in effect taken yourself to the brink of death. If death of your physical body ensues, you will have taken your own life.'

'So this is hell?'

'Hell is a misguided interpretation of the lower astral. **This** *is the lower astral plane. Some may see it as hell. It is the first level of the astral world and those who have light in their soul will not stay here long before moving through to the higher levels.'*

'But Beth didn't take her own life. And her soul is so bright it sometimes blinds me. So why is she here?'

'Because she's coated in evil that is clinging to her like treacle. Darkness will always seek out the light in its effort to become that light. Her brightness is hidden under a cloud of darkness. But she won't linger long on this level. It is why time is important. Time itself does not exist here as we know it, but the light in her soul will propel her towards the higher level without much delay. The coating of darkness clinging to her will not survive the light and will decay quickly.'

Mike felt a subtle change in the atmosphere and blinked as he thought the midnight black had turned to a subtle charcoal grey.

A tall shadow reared up directly in front of him, sending him backwards as his hand flew up in front of his face, startled by the sudden appearance. It was a shadow that had human form, but it had no face, no features, just a shadow that appeared to have density. It swayed in front of him and as suddenly as it appeared, it moved on.

'Astral corpse,' muttered Mam Thomas. *'Just a shell. It has no consciousness and will decay atom by atom over a period of time. Its soul has moved on to a higher plane. Ignore it.'*

There was another change, an overpowering odour of bad drains. In his physical body Mike would have gagged at the stench, but in his astral form it was just another change. It was what it heralded that sent him reeling.

A slow sucking sound entered his consciousness. A slow sucking sound that was getting nearer.

Out of the greyness a huge grey slug, almost half his size was sliming its way towards him. To his abject horror the giant slug possessed a human face. And it was working its oozing jaws in a parody of speech.

Mike clapped his hands over his ears and quickly realised for the second time that sound on the lower astral had a different nature. There was no blocking it out as it taunted him and projected images of vile corruption into his psyche.

Mam Thomas watched him intently as he battled to regain his focus. He suddenly stood tall and erect and addressed the foul creature in front of him.

'I have no business with you or you with me. Get away from me!'

The slug lowered its hideous face and the slow sucking sound resumed as it moved away leaving its stinking slime trail in its wake.

Mam Thomas nodded her approval.

Mike suddenly became aware that they had obviously been travelling without him realising it. She connected with his confusion.

'Intention and thought here are enough to bring about movement.'

The charcoal greyness ahead was broken by the appearance of what seemed like heat haze on hot tarmac, confined to a small area about a hundred feet ahead of them. It shimmered and moved with blue sparks that pierced the dark and Mike could feel its magnetic pull on his solar plexus.

'The gate,' she said simply.

CHAPTER THIRTY THREE: ON THE ASTRAL PLANE

A figure was suddenly approaching them and as it came closer, he could see her. Beth! His thoughts made him accelerate instantly towards her, his arms wide, oblivious to Mam Thomas screaming into his consciousness.

As he took her into his astral arms she leaned into him and put her arms around his neck.

'I knew you'd come for me. I knew you wouldn't abandon me.'

She pulled him in closer to her and whispered to him.

'We can stay here, the two of us, and you'll never feel pain again. You feel no physical pain here, see?'

She reached down to his leg where pain was a constant companion and he realised for the first time that indeed, he could feel no physical pain.

'If we stay here, you'll never feel pain again. You'll be free. We'll both be free. It's beautiful over there, look.' She pointed into the distance.

The greyness faded away at the edge of his astral sight into a lush green valley with forested sides and a crystal river running along its length.

'We can stay here, just the two of us, feeling no pain. Forever.'

He felt a warm glow in his leg and watched as it straightened itself. No pain. His life would be so different. He would be able to look after her and their daughter … their daughter!

Mike made a swift movement backwards, shaking his head and shouting, *'Get away from me! Whoever or whatever you are, you're not her!'*

The sound of cruel laughter vibrated inside him and in that instant there was a lightning bolt of pain in his knee that made it give way and send him crashing to what he perceived as the ground.

'Well done, boy. I thought for a minute ...'

Mam Thomas stood over him as he struggled to stand upright again as the pain burned into him as though it was birthed in the flames of hell. He fought for his breath and screamed in agony.

'I thought there was no pain here!'

'Who told you that? I didn't tell you that. Whatever it was, it was here to tempt you into a life of no pain to prevent you passing through the gate. You consciously chose pain over illusion. There will be no physical pain on the other side.'

By desperate conscious thought he moved forward into the gateway.

And was repelled by the energy vibrating throughout the gateway.

He stood back from it and hurled himself towards it, sending blue sparks into the gloom like a fly that had been zapped and was once again repelled by the shimmering energy.

Frustration and bitter anger flooded him. He turned to the old woman desperate for her help.

'I can't get through! Why? I'm not worthy to pass to the next level? Is that it?'

Mam Thomas shook her head. *'All souls are worthy. But you have a heap of harmful emotions that you must leave behind to enter the next level. You must let go of your anger and bitterness, and your hatred. Drop them like dirty laundry. You still harbour dark thoughts, about those that have taken her and brought her to this. It isn't for you to judge and sanction. It will be done, but not by you. That is not why you are here. It's your darkest thoughts and emotions that are preventing you from passing through.'*

'How? How the hell can I do that?'

'We all come to it differently, but in the end we all have to do it. It's easier for some than others.'

Mike closed his eyes and tried to force all the heavy weight of his hatred and anger away from him, but they hung around him like dark rain clouds. His frustration just served to make them close in again. He felt his anger return, and then in the distance he heard a baby crying and his focus was instantly readjusted.

He took a step forwards, bathing in the soft vibration that flowed within the gateway.

But he could go no further.

Frustration swamped him yet again. He stood within the gateway, looking out at the other side. It was a twilight world of softness and gentle shadows, with pin points of light scattered throughout. He tried to move forwards, but still he remained within the gateway.

A point of light ahead of him began to grow in size and intensity and very slowly began moving towards him.

It grew even brighter as the voice from within it made him choke with emotion.

His mother said, *'There is one hurt and anger that has blossomed into something dark. One that you refuse to acknowledge. Your father. Michael it was I who had the affair. It was I that walked away. It wasn't him. He chose to carry the burden of blame so that you wouldn't hate me while I was dying. He wanted you to remember me as a good mother and faithful wife. His pain over the years has been almost unbearable. You placed me on a pedestal I didn't deserve and denied him of your love for all these years. You must fix it.'*

He reached out towards the light that was encompassing the voice he had loved and lost and as he touched it he felt the love again. The image of his father, alone and frail, was in front of him and it was too much.

Too bloody much.

In that fraction of time he felt the hold of the energy within the gateway release him and he stepped out into the twilight of the next level. Mam Thomas was still at his side.

Mike turned to her. *'What are all those lights?'*

*'Bright souls travelling towards the light of the next level. It is their light that is breaking up the darkness. You have to look for **her** light.'*

'How will I know?'

'*You'll know. You will recognise her own light; you just have to look with your heart not your astral eyes.*'

They moved forwards together as he scanned the wave of travelling lights. In the far distance one light was stilled. He knew in his own soul that it was Beth. As he reached out to her, the tiny pin point of light seemed to shimmer and then it suddenly dipped. Mam Thomas took his arm urgently. '*You have to hurry, she's about to cross!*'

The urgency in her voice resonating inside his head propelled him forwards calling her name into the twilight.

'*I can't see her now!*' His voice in the old woman's head was filled with panic and fear.

Mam Thomas was silent.

As he moved forwards into the vastness of the half light he became aware of the sound of moving water. He followed the rippling vibration and in the distance the silver reflection of a river imprinted itself on his astral eyes.

'*It's the second gate*', she said quietly. *If she reaches the other side, there will be no coming back.*'

Mike ploughed ahead, focussed only on the silver ribbon of light that flowed across his line of sight. The bank was firm and solid and in front of him the river stretched away into the distance, a wide flow of dancing water. He stepped down into it and descended as far as his waist. The current was stronger than he'd expected and in his insubstantial astral form he had to fight against it to keep his feet and to move forwards.

Towards the shimmering light that he knew was her.

He called her name but the light continued to move towards the other side as he fought the current, desperate to gain ground, ploughing forwards. He was half way across and suddenly it was lighter, brighter and he could see her as she travelled in what appeared to be narrow canoe like structures.

She was lying, dreamlike against the bow of the tiny boat, trailing her hand in the fast moving silver river, moving ever onwards towards the opposite bank. Mike felt the panic rise in him again and he struggled to regain the calm that he knew would be his only hope of reaching her.

Mam Thomas was beside him again, and he blinked as she appeared to emit brightness akin to the lights he'd seen. He pulled away from her as she tried to halt him.

'You won't be able to reach her in time. I'll break the rules and slow her progress. When you reach her, you must remember, it has to be her choice. And if she decides to return with you, you have to carry her back across this river and go back without me.'

'What do you mean?'

'He promised a life for a life. I'm not coming back with you.'

The weight of understanding descended on him. *'You never intended to.'*

She shook her head and smiled at him. *'I'm an old woman who has lived a long and contended life. And I am grateful for the chance to enter the light. I can read you. It isn't sacrifice as you see it; it's the natural progression of the soul. I know you have many questions, ask Dai Bricks when you return, he will tell you what you need to know.'*

And she was gone.

Even tears on the astral were different and as his poured down his face, they had evaporated before reaching his chin. He pushed forwards against the surging water. Towards the tiny boat that had almost reached the opposite bank.

The bright light that was the old woman alighted on the other side in front of Beth and immediately became the tall, spare woman, with iron grey hair pulled tight into the nape of her neck, and as Mike pushed on towards them, she stepped into the water and pushed the tiny boat away from the bank.

He reached out his hand and grabbed it.

'Beth?'

She smiled at him. *'What kept you?'*

'Oh, you know, this and that. You ready to come home now? It's kind of a long way.'

No it isn't,' she said.

CHAPTER THIRTY FOUR: REPERCUSSIONS

In the crashing silence of the satanic temple Gavin Radford became aware of Kath Dickinson's hands on him. He opened his eyes and pushed her away roughly.

"Get your stupid self off me, you pathetic bitch!"

She crawled towards him. "Gavin, I'm sorry. It wasn't my fault. We can try again. It doesn't have to be her."

He was yelling now. "Of course it does you silly cow! I promised her to him. … Oh fuck!"

His eyes were fixed on the slimy mass in front of the altar in which a plume of smoke was spiralling upwards.

He ran to the door and yanked on the handle that was held firm by the boards and nails that Jim James had hammered home, banging on it frantically, sweat pooling in the neck of his robe.

The smoke began to thicken and writhe in a hypnotic dance. Kath Dickinson's eyes were firmly fixed on a point about a foot from the top of the pillar of smoke that was taking shape.

He was naked and his face was covered in pustules and set in a grimace of unspeakable horror. He wore a crown on his head and in his left hand he held a writhing, hissing, viper. As she stood transfixed, the body of a dragon had formed beneath him.

Astaroth had returned.

And he was pissed off.

Radford felt his heart rate do the hundred yard dash and kept his eyes averted from the terrible face of the vengeful demon. Covering his ears with his hands as the sound of Kath Dickinson being consumed burned itself into his memory, never to be erased.

There seemed no thought process involved as he threw himself across the room and hurled himself towards the far corner where a tapestry depicting a goat, seated cross legged with a flame between its horns and an arm raised in a blasphemous salute, hung against the wall.

He snatched at the edge and pulled it aside as the demon's derisive laugh thundered throughout the room and beyond. The door behind the tapestry was low and small but opened easily as he turned the twisted iron ring handle, into the second priest hole.

The tunnel was dark and narrow and he tore his robe in several places as his large frame scraped against the rough hewn stones. His scalp was bleeding into rivulets of red that ran down his face as his head continually collided with the roof of the tunnel as he frantically kept looking over his shoulder.

In a small bedroom at the end of the corridor, Jim James had stood vigil over three inert forms. He'd been unaware of their intentions but as he had hurried the others out of the abbey, Dai Bricks had stopped him.

"You need to stay here, look. Need to keep an eye on them as they travels, isn't it. Make sure nothin' comes for 'em while they're travelling."

He'd looked perplexed and Dai had told him of Mam Thomas's intentions. It was the day for stretching his belief systems until their knicker elastic snapped. He shut out the nagging thoughts of boards of enquiry, internal investigations and loss of pension and ran hell for leather back up the stairs praying his cholesterol levels would hold off the heart attack as he burst into the small room where Mike, Beth and Mam Thomas appeared waxwork-like in a tableau of tragedy.

Dai had told him on no account to try and wake them, that he had to let events take their course, that whatever happened, he had to trust in something beyond himself.

As Mike had journeyed in his astral body, his physical self had tossed and turned and on two separate occasions his low murmurings had changed into blood curdling cries that had created more grey hairs on Jim's head.

The first time it happened, Jim understood what was meant by ones testicles retracting into the body. He felt his practically hit his prostate. He would be eternally grateful that he hadn't pissed himself.

Mam Thomas and Beth had remained still and silent, his eyes had remained fixed firmly on Mike, willing him to do whatever, wherever, and get the hell back into his body.

From the silence of the world outside the bedroom there was a frantic pounding. He knew immediately. Gavin St John Radford was looking for the way out. He turned to the still, silent figures, did he go and look? Did he let the bastard find a way out? What happened to Dai's theory that some inhabitant of the outer reaches of hell would come for them? How much of it had been bullshit? Bullshit he'd listened to. The tentacles of creeping doubt reached into his rational mind. What the fuck was he doing there? He should have arrested the bastard and be done with it. He took a step towards the door, stopping in his tracks as the sickening sounds that he shouldn't have been able to hear, echoed in his inner ears. Then the unholy laughter reverberated throughout the abbey.

Okay. Decision made. He'd stay put.

But he was going to have a serious talk with Dai Bricks. Git.

Mike and Beth stirred and opened their eyes. Jim's relief was intense and overwhelming as he helped them to their feet.

He looked over at the still form of Mam Thomas expectantly.

Mike's face was granite as he shook his head.

CHAPTER THIRTY FIVE: PROTECT THE CHILD

In the sunlit living room of Brookstone Cottage Jack's face still portrayed the shock he felt. He paced up and down trying to make sense of the illogical, the unreasonable, the damn near impossible and he was getting nowhere.

Dai Bricks was sitting in an armchair saying nothing, waiting until Jack had finished pacing. He would wait for the best part of half an hour.

Martha had bathed the baby who was sleeping fitfully, wrapped in a soft white shawl. She rocked the child gently, trying to induce sleep that wouldn't come until she would be safe in Beth's arms.

Eventually Jack stopped pacing and sat opposite Dai.

"So, now what?"

"Now I have to go and find Ruby Thomas, someone's got to tell her old Maggie's passed over."

"So let's get this straight, she …"

He was interrupted as the spectral appearance of Adain seemed to materialise next to Martha and he watched spell bound as she put a hand on Martha's arm and appeared to whisper into her ear. Martha's expression was stone as she nodded her apparent understanding. As suddenly as she had appeared Adain was gone.

Jack stood up quickly. "What the f …?"

"I just need to get something from my boxes," Martha replied, heading for the door.

Dai Bricks held up his hand to Jack who was about to follow her.

"She knows what she's about, boy. Leave it."

Jack sat down heavily, "So I just sit here? Come on, there must be something I can do!"

207

"Stay here with them. I have to go."

Martha reappeared still cradling the child in the shawl as Dai pulled his cap firmly onto his head and left.

"We need to talk," Martha said sternly. What she meant was, *I need to talk and you need to listen.*

Jack obeyed without hesitation.

Minutes seemed like hours as they waited and watched the hands of the long case clock. They didn't seem to move.

Then suddenly, Martha tensed visibly.

There was a loud crash and the sound of splintering wood and Gavin St John Radford was striding towards them, dried blood lining his face, caked mud still clinging to his torn robe.

He threw his hands in the air, piercing Jack with coal black eyes rendering him still and silent as he had done in the temple. He was on a high of returning dark power and he knew what to do with it. Jack was helpless.

Martha pulled the baby closer to her chest.

"Give her to me old woman."

Martha didn't move.

"Give her to me now." The tone of his voice had changed and had become hypnotic and almost seductive.

Martha lifted her arms and took a step forwards.

And handed the soft white bundle to him, his face triumphant. He would be exonerated in the eyes of Astaroth.

There was a loud bang and a bewildered expression appeared on Radford's face as he fell to the floor, a black hole between his eyes.

Jack leaped to his feet, Martha's pistol in his hand.

Martha bent over Radford and retrieved the shawl and the pillow inside it before it was contaminated further. Upstairs, little Adain was crying at the sound of the gunshot.

"Vermin. Made a mess of the carpet."

Jack swayed and dashed into the kitchen to vomit into

the sink.

"Reminded me of Jethro Hobbs. Liked to dissect things. Had to expel him in the end."

The regular thrumming of rotor blades overhead silenced them as they went to the window to watch as Mike used all his skills to land the helicopter on the gentle slope down to the brook.

Jim James emerged first, helping the weakened Beth out onto the overgrown lawn. Mike followed, landing heavily on his already painful leg. He grimaced but moved as quickly as he could towards the cottage. He burst in through the glass doors that led out onto the terrace and took in the bizarre scene in front of him, his agile brain processing the visual information. He exhaled loudly.

"It's over," he said in a hoarse whisper.

Beth's voice from behind him seemed to come from far away. "No. It isn't," she said.

Martha went to her and laid the infant in her arms, swallowing hard as Beth buried her head in the shawl and wept. Jack looked away and cleared his throat.

"You guys really know how to throw a party."

Jim James was white faced, looking down at Radford's body. "Oh for Christ's sake! How the hell am I supposed to …I don't even want to know. But I'll clear it up. Don't know how, but I'll clear it up."

Beth raised her tear stained face from the shawl and kissed her daughter lovingly on her soft downy head. "Hello," was all she could manage.

Martha sniffed loudly. "I'll put the kettle on."

"No!" Beth had pulled herself together. "There's something we have to do right now."

They looked at her with puzzled expressions. Mike put his arm around her shoulders and tried to guide her towards the sofa. She shook her head.

"She's been touched by evil, baptised and dedicated to the demon Astaroth. She's tainted. She needs to be re-baptised. Now."

Without further speech she stepped out onto the terrace and slowly walked towards the brook, skirting the helicopter with firm footsteps. Mike was right behind her, followed by Martha and Jack.

At the edge of the brook Adain stood watching with a tall young man at her side.

Beth stepped into the bubbling shallow water and bent down, whispering softly to her daughter, and praying. She cupped her hand and dipped it into the crystal clear brook and poured the pure water over the baby's head.

"I adjure all evil and renounce the devil and all his works. I baptise you into the realms of light and name you Adain, Martha, Maggie. May God bless you and keep you."

Mike was biting down hard on his bottom lip, Martha had her jaws clamped tightly together and Jack was crying unashamedly, his shoulders shaking as Beth handed Adain to him.

"Meet your Godfather, sweetheart."

Jack couldn't speak.

Mike lifted the child from his arms and handed her to Martha, "And your Godmother," he said as he planted a kiss on Martha's forehead.

He turned to Beth, "*Now* you're going to bed."

"In a minute," she said softly. She turned to the opposite bank, where Adain was still watching them. Beth raised her hand. "We'll see to it, I promise. You'll have a proper burial and we'll make it known what happened to you and hopefully clear Owain's name. I heard you say that Llewellyn's locket is still in your hand; it's evidence. You can move on now. Thank you for everything."

Adain raised her hand in farewell and the two of them began walking into the forest. She stood at the edge of the tall pines and waved again before they slowly dissolved into the trees.

Beth pulled Adain closer and nodded, leaning against Mike as he painfully guided her back into the cottage.

CHAPTER THIRTY SIX: AFTERMATH

Mike, Jack and Martha sat huddled together on the sofa as Jim went to the door, returning almost instantly accompanied by Dai Bricks, Geraint Meredith and Ruby Thomas.

They watched in silence as Dai and Geraint lifted the body of Gavin St John Radford and hauled him outside to toss him unceremoniously into the back of Dai's van.

Dai was the first to come back into the room.

"Plenty of old mine shafts over Blaenavon way. Geraint's going to see to it. Says it's all his fault, won't listen to reason."

The others returned seconds later as Beth came through the doorway.

"She's fed and asleep," she said as Jack shot up off the sofa for her to sit down. She nestled into Mike who let his head rest on top of hers.

Jack couldn't hold back any longer. He looked around at the others.

"So who *are* you people?"

No one spoke.

"*Well?*"

Dai cleared his throat. "Well me and old Maggie Thomas and Brian Jenkins, we're what they call Watchers. Keeping an eye out for anything or anyone coming back, like. Coming back from the dark where they belong. Been doing it for thirty years now, old Maggie a hell of a lot longer." He paused, and then laughed aloud, "Spiritual warriors is how Brian Jenkins sees it. Me and Maggie, well, we thought we were more like housekeepers. Keeping things in their proper place, see. Dealing with the crap and cleaning up, like."

Jack shook his head.

"So why did you let things get out of hand? Why didn't you stop it before it started?"

"Don't work that way. We're not allowed to interfere, just watch. Allowed to guide anyone who asks for it though. Free will, isn't it? Every soul has its own destiny and path, has to be allowed to make its own choices. When they makes the wrong ones, then we do what's needed to keep the good guys safe and clean up the mess after."

Martha nodded. "Read about that in one of my old books. Seems reasonable."

Jack was on a roll.

"*Reasonable? Reasonable?* Am I the only one who thinks the worlds tilted on its axis or something? How can any of this be reasonable? Oh, I know! This isn't happening, is it? It's not real. I'm gonna wake up with the mother of a hangover, take some aspirin, throw up and it'll all go away."

Martha stood up and took Jack's arm. "Come with me."

Jack immediately felt the indignity of standing outside the headmistress's office.

"You ..." she began.

"Don't tell me," he replied, "I remind you of some spotty kid who wouldn't do his homework!"

She snorted, "Something like that. I'm going to make tea. You, I suspect will make use of the whisky decanter. Make sure Michael gets a large one." She let go of his arm, but the warning look in her eye relayed its own message.

Geraint and Ruby were making for the door. Mike stood up and put his hand on Geraint's arm. "Are you okay? It really wasn't your fault, you know."

A bashful smile played around Geraint's mouth. "I'm okay." He nodded towards Ruby. "Going to marry me, isn't she. Says all I need is a good woman. No kids' stuff, nothing soppy or anything like that. Good friends we are, makes sense."

Mike smiled at him. "Makes more sense than anything else that's happened. Good on you." He clapped him on the back and walked with them to the door.

When he returned, Jack was handing him a half full tumbler of amber liquid. "Cheers, Spooky," he said. "So it was the consecrated communion wafer that did for Astaroth? Power of the church and all that."

Beth shook her head. "No. It was the power of your mother's love contained in it that did for him. Demons can't stand against love."

Dai stood up, turning his cap in his hand, "There's one more thing, see. With old Mam Thomas gone, like, there's a bit of a gap to fill. So, I was wondering …"

The silence seemed to stretch into eternity.

Then Mike said simply, "I'll do it."

Beth was about to protest, then thought better of it and kissed him on the forehead. It would always be that way with him. He wasn't destined for a peaceful life, but she'd do her damnedest to minimise the fallout.

He stood up and went to the kitchen and rummaged in his jacket for his phone. He dialled and waited.

"Dad? It's Mike. I … I… I wanted to tell you that you have a daughter in law, and you're a grandfather. Dad, I'm sorry."

Whatever his father said to him would always remain between them, but the healing had begun. Beth smiled.

His phone rang in his hand and he tossed it to Jack and went back to Beth. He wasn't taking any calls.

After a few minutes Jack returned. "Bloke on the phone wants you, Mike. Say's his name's Josh someone or other, says you knew him in university. Says he needs to speak to you urgently. I told him I'd see if you were in."

Mike shrugged and went into the kitchen. Jim James and Dai were about to take their leave when Jim turned to Martha.

"I need to have a chat about the gun. Tomorrow will

213

do."

Martha raised her eyebrows. "Really young man, I have absolutely no idea what you're talking about."

Jim met her flinty stare, smiled and raised his hands in the air. "Whatever. I'm going to the pub."

Mike's voice drifted in through the open door.

"Hi, this is Mike." He listened quietly. "Yes, I remember you. Got yourself into hot water with a paper you wrote as I remember it."

He listened in silence for several minutes, then, ashen, he exclaimed, "The Ark of the *what?*"

END.

THANK YOU!

To my Reader:

Many thanks for buying *Long Shadows*, I hope you enjoyed reading it.

If you did enjoy it, please post a review at Amazon, Goodreads or your favourite social network site and let your friends know about *Long Shadows*.

I hope that this has whetted your appetite to read the other novels in the Mike Travis paranormal investigation series. You can find details of these in the next few pages as well as the short stories collection: *Beginnings*.

Happy Reading!
All the best
Jan

ALSO BY JAN MCDONALD

BEGINNINGS

MIKE TRAVIS
PARANORMAL INVESTIGATIONS

MIKE TRAVIS
PARANORMAL INVESTIGATOR

BROOKSTONE COTTAGE, BROOKSTONE,
MONMOUTH, S. WALES

JAN
McDONALD

BEGINNINGS

A bonus of five short stories for fans of the Mike Travis
paranormal investigations

It all began for Mike Travis with a helicopter crash in war-
torn Afghanistan that resulted in his being declared
clinically dead; before expert combat medics brought him
back to life.
But he came back with a gift. He could see ghosts.
These five short stories bridge the gap between what
happened in the immediate aftermath of the crash to his
arrival in Crowsmoor, Cornwall, where his help has been
summoned in an effort to prevent the return of an ancient
evil.
Beginnings charts his progress from his first encounter
with a ghost to his becoming a recognised investigator into
all things paranormal. For readers of the series, these five
short stories will be familiar territory.

*If you have a smartphone, you can buy Beginnings at Amazon by
scanning the barcode below:*

HALLOWEEN

MIKE TRAVIS
PARANORMAL INVESTIGATIONS

JAN
McDONALD

HALLOWEEN

A bonus of four Mike Travis short stories for Halloween

Halloween – or All Hallows' Eve: A night when we can expect murmurings from beyond the veil. Paranormal investigator, Mike Travis, is kept busy keeping spirits and demons away from us at the best of times. But on Halloween he has his work cut out as people meddle with forces that they don't understand.

So once the 'trick or treaters' have gone home, light the fire, turn the lights down and be prepared to see things in the shadows when you read these four seasonal short

If you have a smartphone, you can buy Halloween at Amazon by scanning the barcode below:

THE CROWSMOOR CURSE

MIKE TRAVIS

PARANORMAL INVESTIGATIONS

JAN McDONALD

THE CROWSMOOR CURSE

The dead of Crowsmoor are light sleepers.

Some say they sleep with one eye open, keeping watch over the restless ones.

When Beth Trevithick is sent as parish priest to the isolated and scattered community of Crowsmoor, in the middle of bleak Bodmin Moor, Cornwall, she finds a community entrenched in fear and superstition and belief in an ancient curse born of dark magic.

She gets unexpected help in the form of Mike Travis, ex RAF helicopter pilot medically discharged after crashing in war torn Afghanistan, he has turned to his other love, the paranormal, devoting all of his time to paranormal investigation.

Beth soon discovers the fear and superstition in Crowsmoor are well founded and together with Mike fights for her own sanity and her life.

If you have a smartphone, you can buy The Crowsmoor Curse at Amazon by scanning the barcode below:

THE
SACRED
ARK

MIKE TRAVIS

PARANORMAL INVESTIGATIONS

JAN
McDONALD

THE SACRED ARK

A longer pause and then a lowered tone.
"Jesus Christ, Josh. What have you found?"
An even longer pause.
"The Ark of the Covenant."

When paranormal investigator Mike Travis answers a call
for help, he doesn't anticipate being flung headlong into
Ancient Egyptian secrets in *The Sacred Ark*. An old
acquaintance needs his help in his search for proof that his
controversial theories are correct, theories which have
resulted in him being ridiculed by the world of
archaeology.

Mike finds himself in the heart of the Sinai desert pursued
by government and Vatican hit men, all desperate to find
the same thing, the Ark of the Covenant. What secrets
does it hide and where will it take him?

*If you have a smartphone, you can buy The Sacred Ark at Amazon
by scanning the barcode below:*

THE
HAUNTED DIARY OF
VICTORIA LITTLE
MIKE TRAVIS
PARANORMAL INVESTIGATIONS
JAN
McDONALD

THE HAUNTED DIARY OF VICTORIA LITTLE

*I have read the diary from cover to cover and now I wonder if there is
an element of reality in what she has written and that in fact the
truth is more terrifying than anything she could imagine.
I have enclosed her diary so that you can decide for yourself whether or
not there is something happening that would explain her situation
and perhaps even find some small way to help her. I am sure that
somewhere inside her is the mother that I once knew.*

When Mike Travis stays at home to finish writing his next
book he doesn't expect to be embroiled in a new case.
A mysterious letter and diary are sent to him and he soon
finds himself battling ancient demons with the help of
friends old and new.
He believes that Victoria Little is the victim of possession
rather than mental illness and sets out to free her and rid
her of the vicious demon Ahriman. The fight takes him
into the world of ancient dark magic which has stretched
its legacy into lives past and present.
Who is connected to this ancient evil and which side of the
Abyss do they live on? Who can he trust?

*If you have a smartphone, you can buy The Haunted Diary of
Victoria Little at Amazon by scanning the barcode below:*

THE MERLIN MANUSCRIPT

Paranormal Investigator Mike Travis's day is about to get way past difficult. His friend, Jack Carter, has been kidnapped, and it all revolves around an old manuscript that was supposedly a copy of one made by Merlin himself before he was magically cast into a crystal cave by his lover and student, Nimue.

Who has Jack? And where is he?

The trail leads Mike to the Inquisition, alive and well on the fringes of the Vatican, with their reaches in his own neighbourhood. They want the manuscript and what it refers to – Merlin and Excalibur. And they'll do whatever they have to, to obtain their ends.

To save Jack, Mike has to journey back through the veil to Avalon accompanied by Benjamin Lovecraft, ex Catholic Priest and Exorcist, to claim Excalibur and find Merlin. The worlds of magic and legend collide to draw Mike into a quest that leads him to find more than a magician and a sword.

If you have a smartphone, you can buy The Crowsmoor Curse at Amazon by scanning the barcode below:

MIDNIGHT WINE

JAN MCDONALD

MIDNIGHT WINE

Ex Catholic priest, Beckett, is out for blood. Vampire blood.

History is repeating itself and Beckett enlists the help of Dr Lane Dearing, herself a powerful vampire, in an effort to save the beautiful Katerini from a sadistic and vicious Undead. Their struggle leads them from the mysterious mountains of the Brecon Beacons in Wales to an isolated monastery in rural Greece where they encounter one of the Ancient Ones who has his own reasons for wanting Katerini.

Midnight Wine is a vampire tale of love, revenge and sacrifice. Vampires are real. They exist.
And they are out there...

If you have a smartphone, you can buy Midnight Wine at Amazon by scanning the barcode below:

FROM THE AUTHOR OF
MIDNIGHT WINE

LYCAN
JAN MCDONALD

LYCAN

Acceptance didn't sit well with ex-Catholic priest Beckett.
And being a vampire wasn't going to come easy. Struggling
with his new life he finds himself helping another whose
life has been dramatically changed. Jude Mason is suffering
from Post Traumatic Stress Disorder; but Beckett and the
elegant vampire Lane Dearing believe that there is more to
it.
Much more.
Their efforts to understand and help the man are
hampered by unfinished business. In the tiny monastery in
Greece, where they believed they had ended the killing
spree of ruthless and savage vampires, one has survived.
They must return to finish what began years previously
with the death of the beautiful newly turned vampire,
Katerini.
In Greece, there is as much to lose as to be won and with
the stakes high someone has to pay the price.

*If you have a smartphone, you can buy Lycan at Amazon by
scanning the barcode below:*

CONTACT DETAILS

Visit the authors website:
jan-mcdonald.co.uk

Follow on Twitter:
www.twitter.com/janmcdonald1

Cover designed by: Raven Crest Books
Cover photography © viperagp - Fotolia.com

Published by: Raven Crest Books
www.ravencrestbooks.com

Follow us on Facebook:
www.facebook.com/ravencrestbooksclub